A FAMILY SECRET

Symons Hill is a charming, close-knit Australian town, where April Stewart's happiness is linked to Symon Andrews of the area's pioneering family. When he leaves suddenly for the city, rumours abound. Heartbroken, April immerses herself in her animal refuge work until he returns unexpectedly. Though he reawakens her feelings, his actions threaten to change the relaxed character of Symons Hill. What has happened to change this once warm, thoughtful man, and how will April learn the truth?

JO JAMES

A FAMILY SECRET

Complete and Unabridged

LINFORD
Leicester

First published in Great Britain in 2005

First Linford Edition
published 2006

British Library CIP Data

James, Jo
    A family secret.—Large print ed.—
Linford romance library
1. Love stories
2. Large type books
I. Title
823.9′2 [F]

ISBN 1–84617–266–7

Published by
F. A. Thorpe (Publishing)
Anstey, Leicestershire

Set by Words & Graphics Ltd.
Anstey, Leicestershire
Printed and bound in Great Britain by
T. J. International Ltd., Padstow, Cornwall

This book is printed on acid-free paper

1

April Stewart lengthened her stride on her morning walk to the post office. Basil, her black labrador, strained at the leash, encouraging her to better her pace. As the early autumn sun touched her bare arms and legs, she felt almost back to her normal, positive self.

Soon she and Basil jogged along the verge of the unsealed bush track which led to the main road. She hadn't been running regularly in a long time. It was two, possibly three years, since her jogging partner walked away. The fact that she didn't know to the day how long it was meant, she hoped, she'd finally consigned Symon Andrews to the past.

And to convince herself, she promised Basil with a smile, 'From now on, we'll do it every day. In future you'll be my faithful running mate. Who needs a man when they can have someone as dependable and uncomplicated as you?' She spoke it without a choke in her voice, tension in her stomach. Symon Andrews was history.

Punching the air, she added, 'You're getting fat, my friend.' Basil barked, surged forward, reminding her she'd been the slack one.

She pushed herself. Her trainers hardly seemed to touch the ground, her limbs felt loose. Loose and free of the emotional baggage she'd carried since Symon left without so much as a goodbye.

At the top of Red Gum track, she turned left into the main road which led to her small township. Breathing hard, she paused to let a car pass. Basil scratched around in the carpet of autumn leaves. But soon they crossed the bitumen and took off again.

Bob Daniels gave her a wave and the thumbs-up sign from his car as it passed. She waved back, hardly able to figure out how easily she'd slipped back into running. On a high, she announced to the world, 'From now on I'm going to be a winner. Winners are grinners.'

On reaching the post office, she bent briefly to recover her breath before securing Basil's lead to a post outside the nearby general store.

'If old Mrs Jackson goes by carrying her umbrella, you mustn't bark. She thinks you're growling at her,' she warned him.

Then she tackled the drooping fly-wire door of the peeling weatherboard building attached to Ruth Henderson's house. Every day she promised herself she'd ask Bob Daniels to repair it, every day, in keeping with all the other residents, she carefully unlatched it, eased it open, left after a chat and promptly forgot about it.

For years the building had served as the post office, the hub of the small community. Ruth, a widow, ran it. Similar to the post office itself, she was regarded as a local treasure. The mail didn't go astray for Ruth knew everyone who lived in town, moved into the area or farmed in the outlying areas. Let's face it, April amended with amusement, she's the eyes and ears of Symons Hill, but she's never indiscreet.

The door shuddered and screeched closed behind her, but the racket didn't prompt Ruth to look up and greet her as she usually did. The postmistress continued sorting letters into pigeon holes.

'Wow,' April said brightly to gain her attention. 'I've just run the Olympic fifteen hundred metres in my personal best for years.'

Ruth turned slowly around, a bundle of letters in one hand. 'You're glowing,' she commented, but her usual smile failed to emerge.

'You're obviously not. Problems, Ruthie?'

The older woman swept a wisp of greying hair from her face. 'I've had the phone call I've been dreading. I'm about to lose the post office.'

April took a step forward, frowned.

'Come on, Ruth, Symons Hill without its post office? Australia without the outback?' She raised her shoulders. 'Huh. Not even thinkable.'

Tears welled in Ruth's normally cheerful eyes, her elbows slumped across the counter. 'It is and it's about to happen.'

April reached over to touch her friend's arm. 'How can you be so sure?'

Ruth dabbed at her eyes with a tissue, said testily, 'Because I've been told.'

'I can't believe it. You must be shattered. I know how much the job means to you.'

'It's my bread and butter, but what's more important, while I run the business from here, I can keep Mum with me.' She lowered her voice. 'I don't want this to be common knowledge for her sake, but her Alzheimers is developing quicker than I'd hoped. She's inclined to wander off or do odd things if I don't keep tabs on her all the time. She forgets what she's doing.'

'I'm so sorry. Can I help in some way?'

Ruth didn't seem to hear. 'At least in here Mum can sit with me and talk to the customers. It fills in her day and I know where she is all the time. If I have to give this up and find another job . . . ' She broke off, wiped at a tear. 'I'd hate for her to have to go to a nursing home. She'd never settle, and I want to care for her as long as I can.'

'I'm sure it's going to be all right. We have to receive our mail, I mean, this isn't your average Australian suburb. We don't have the luxury of postal deliveries to the houses. Besides, it's the most convenient place for people, particularly the older folk, to pay their utilities and phone bills and do their banking. Australia Post wouldn't cut us off at the knees by closing the post office.'

April sounded confident, but in fact doubts had begun to cloud the happiness with which she'd started out this morning.

'Didn't I explain?' Ruth said, her voice

flat. 'They're not closing it, it's being transferred to the store. The new owner moves in in two weeks and the postal authorities have decided it's more economical to give the operating licence to the shop. That's progress for you. Heaven help me, what on earth am I going to do?' She sank her head into her hands.

April was furious. 'What a nerve. It's our post office. It's an integral part of our community and no-one thought to consult us? Don't give up yet, Ruthie, we'll get a petition going. I can't imagine Symons Hill without post-mistress, Ruth Henderson. Make that postperson,' she amended, in the futile hope it might ease the grim lines on Ruth's face.

April's sombre mood began to pick up as a steady flow of adrenalin through her veins triggered her mind into planning mode. A tussle with the authorities to retain Symons Hill as a rural haven on the outskirts of Melbourne, would unite the townsfolk even more.

She wasn't new to this kind of thing. Eighteen months ago she'd been on the committee to save the small primary school, and they'd won that battle. After numerous rallies and sit-ins, media publicity, and the arrival of a small family in the area to boost the pupil numbers, the authorities had backed down.

'Remember our fight to keep the school? You won't be tipped out by the bureaucrats, Ruth. I'll call a meeting for tonight, muster the troops. We'll form a *Save the Post Office Committee*.'

'It's generous of you, but I don't think it'll do any good.' With a tissue, Ruth patted the moisture from her red-rimmed eyes.

'Of course it will. The people in Symons Hill won't stand by and watch a stranger buy our store and con Australia Post into granting a licence. That's about as underhand as you can get.'

'Look I wasn't going to say anything, but . . . ' she shrugged, ' . . . but I guess

8

you're going to find out sooner than later. Apparently it wasn't bought by a stranger.'

April frowned. 'You mean a local? Surely that has to be good? He'll — I take it it's a he — will appreciate the problem. He won't accept the licence.'

'The post office official said he already has.'

April put her hands on her hips. 'You're not talking about that mean-spirited Watson guy who moved in with the purpose of bulldozing the wetlands and throwing up ugly little townhouses on the outskirts of town? We soon gave him his marching orders.'

'If only.' Ruth hesitated. 'Er . . . I don't know how to say this, but it's someone you used to know very well, April. Er, it's . . .'

April, with a reassuring smile, cut in. 'Really? An old friend? I'll talk to him, try to persuade him to change his mind. Who is it?'

The sound of Basil's friendly bark broke her concentration. Someone

9

spoke his name. The dog barked again. And suddenly she didn't need to hear Ruth's answer. From behind her came a heart-beatingly familiar voice.

She swung around, eyes wide. The wire door of the post office tipped drunkenly on its hinges, opened, and April came face-to-face with Symon Andrews. She'd once thought him outrageously handsome with honey-gold hair which flopped idly across a wide forehead, light blue eyes which sometimes became almost translucent.

But, a few years back he'd dropped completely out of sight, completely out of her life. And though local people speculated on his departure, she'd never found an answer to satisfy her for his sudden exodus from The Hill.

She'd fallen hard for her jogging partner years, long years ago, and he'd charmed her into believing he cared deeply for her.

'I'm certainly willing to listen to anything you have to say. How are you, April?' He sounded so in control, whereas she had this awful knot in her stomach as all her old uncertainties came rampaging back.

'You,' she shrilled, 'I can't believe you've got the nerve to turn up unannounced like this.'

'I'm fine, thanks. How nice of you to welcome me home and enquire about my health,' he said, his tone laced with sarcasm. 'You're obviously well, judging by the colour in your cheeks.'

His disturbingly light eyes and his words mocked her, but when he dashed his hair back from his face, she knew this mannerism well, she felt uncomfortable. She understood, too, why Ruth looked so tight-lipped.

'Are you saying you bought the store?' she demanded, mopping at sweat under her fringe. She felt like a damp rag yet he looked . . . well, face it, cool, more handsome, more mature than she remembered, as he leaned against the counter. But his looks didn't rate, it was his assumption that he could walk back into their lives and take over as if he'd never been away that really irritated her.

'I hope The Hill hasn't decreed it a hanging offence to go into business since I left. Perhaps that's why things don't look all that prosperous around here.' He studied her, his brows raised in question.

How dare he. 'We were doing very nicely without you, but now you'll have the whole town wondering why you'd buy the store when you've got Symons Run, and you haven't even bothered to make sure it's prospering in years? Your so-called friends haven't received one postcard between the lot of us.'

He jerked up his head as if he'd been struck. She shuffled the mail Ruth handed her, feigning an interest in it, but deeply disturbed by the sudden knowledge that she was surrendering to a sweep of tired, spent and almost forgotten feelings.

'Everyone knows I don't own The Run. It's my grandfather's property.'

She shrugged, lowered her voice.

'Come on, Symon, you're playing with semantics. Everyone also knows it's as good as yours. You're Cyrus Symons' only heir.'

He turned to Ruth. 'Any mail for Grandfather?' he asked.

'That's right, change the subject in your usual evasive way.' April had lost her cool again.

'If you can prove to me you have some stake in knowing what my future prospects are, I'm happy to discuss the matter with you. But from where I stand it clearly has nothing to do with anyone in this town.'

'It'll have a lot to do with the folk if you're relying on them as customers in your store.'

Dear Heaven, she sounded like a shrew. Her fingers flew to her face as if to massage away the heat of embarrassment. Of course his family's wealth had nothing to do with her or anyone else, but right now she'd lost the will to even make an effort to apologise or be conciliatory.

She turned to Ruth. 'I can see there's no point in appealing to Mr Andrews' good nature. He's already shown he's a man who doesn't believe in explaining his actions.'

Swinging back, she faced him again, her heart burning with contempt, which surprised her, for she wasn't normally vindictive.

'I don't think I have anything to explain, but you're free to say what's really bugging you, if it makes you feel better,' he said with the deep, low voice she had once thought could persuade her to do anything.

It wouldn't. Of course it wouldn't. He'd run out on her, abandoned her, and she'd never understood, never found the missing link between their growing relationship and his sudden disappearance. This morning on her jog she'd confidently predicted she was over him. And now? She felt . . . she felt wretched, a loser again, while he remained irritatingly controlled and scored all the ticks. That's what really bugged her. She needed time and space to work through her tangled emotions.

She shifted the weight on her feet. 'I think I've made my point.'

'Good, because I need to get home to polish up my people skills. I had no idea this community felt so resentful towards me.' He dashed hair back from his forehead. Beads of sweat glistened. Cool exterior, probably steaming inside, too, she thought with a vague sense of satisfaction.

Carefully she avoided his eyes, afraid she might find loathing in them as she searched for a way in which to restore some of her pride. She'd carried on like a drama queen, and her behaviour reflected badly on a woman who prided herself on being thoughtful and caring.

'If I've upset you, sorry. Everything that needs to be said will be tonight,' she said, tilting her chin with hard-won determination.

He lounged nonchalantly against the counter, asked in a frustratingly controlled tone, 'Tonight?'

'At the protest meeting.'

'I heard about your fight to save the school. I hope the government isn't trying to shut it down again?'

She talked up a cool reply. 'I'm referring to our meeting to save the post office, our post office.'

And determined to get out before she lost it again, on her way to the door, she brushed by him. She felt the cool flesh of his arm on hers. It burned like the rest of her with indignation.

'You didn't mention the time the meeting gets underway.'

'Eight o'clock,' she snapped as she reached the door, which shimmied, rocked and grumbled on its hinges as she attempted to open it.

He reached out, prevented it from falling against her.

'Sorry, I forgot, Ruth,' she said as he stood beside her holding onto the sagging metal frame. 'I promise, this time I will ask Bob Daniels, or one of the other guys to come up and fix it.'

'It's not necessary, I'm happy to

make some temporary repairs,' Symon said, raising brows, exuding superiority.

Simmering, she ignored the word temporary, but when he added, 'I'll see you at the meeting, April,' that did it.

She turned quickly, narrowed her eyes, shook her head. 'I think not. You're not invited.'

'I was under the impression we still live in a democracy. If it's an open meeting, I'll be there. I'm entitled to a right of reply and I intend to take it.'

She couldn't argue with logic. Besides, if he came tonight he'd get the message loud and clear. Symons Hill people would not stand by and let him make a grab for the post office. Tossing her shoulders she said as evenly as she could, 'At your peril.'

The superior brows shot up again. 'I'll risk it.'

Her laugh tainted with scorn, she replied, 'Don't say I didn't warm you. We love our post office, and we love Ruth. They belong to the people, not the Symons family.'

He caught her glance, pinned her down with amusement shining in his luminous blue eyes. 'I didn't know you were taking drama lessons. Your emotion-charged lines are well done.'

If one thing really roused April's wrath, it was men ridiculing women for being emotional. As if there was something wrong with showing how much you cared on an issue.

'And I don't like the fact that you don't care about this district.'

Turning to Ruth, who throughout the exchange had stood taut, crimson-faced, she said, 'Sorry Ruthie, but it had to be said. I'll ring you later to let you know the plans for tonight.'

'I'll look forward to seeing you again this evening,' Symon said. 'I hope you're in a friendlier mood by then.'

Her heart racing, April gave him a look which she hoped communicated disgust, before storming across to Basil and releasing his lead.

What gave Symon Andrews the idea he could sneak back into The Hill, buy

18

the store and arrange to have the post office transferred into it without a community outcry? Of course the townsfolk would protest. He knew the little post office building had historical significance. That, she assumed, was his motivation for doing the deal in secret. How much of his life had he kept secret, she forced herself to ask. How little had she known him, she started to wonder with concern.

She began to run, hoping to exorcise her anger, her disbelief that he could be so different from the person she'd loved.

'Some people think money can buy them everything,' she harangued Basil, 'but he'll learn a hard lesson tonight. Perhaps for the first time he'll find out money can't buy honesty and integrity.'

Her heart lurched. Until he suddenly left Symons Hill without so much as a note, she'd thought him generous and considerate. She'd hoped he was planning to ask her to be his wife. Now she faced the truth. He'd probably never intended to marry her, never thought her good enough to become a member of his family. He'd probably always possessed the high and mighty, acquisitive nature of his forefathers, who pioneered Symons Run, but she'd been too captivated to see it.

In the late eighteen-hundreds, the first Cyrus Symons had arrived from England and opened up a vast tract of land to the north-east of Melbourne town. The family farmed sheep and prospered. They named the area Symons Run and with the discovery of gold in the area, the small town of Symons Hill developed.

At the vicarage gate, April took several deep breaths to ease the ache of betrayal in her stomach, and forced herself to the door where she knocked. She couldn't falter now.

The vicar, looking over his glasses, greeted her with a smile. 'Come in, my dear, I believe you're here about a meeting you're planning.'

It brought a smile to her lips. 'This

town's communication system leaves e-mail in the shade. Did Ruth ring?'

'Ruth confided her problem to me earlier, and when I saw you on your way to the post office, I guessed what would result, so I gave her a call.'

Again April smiled. 'Did you guess we'd need the parish hall, and I want you to chair the meeting, too?'

'I checked. The hall's free tonight but, my dear, I'm suggesting Rod Marsh would be a more appropriate chairperson.'

Rod, the primary school principal, had arrived in town late last year after the retirement of the long-time head-master, and April soon found herself warming to him. He'd started a small book reading group, which she'd joined, and sometimes together they visited a restaurant or the theatre in the city. Sometimes Ruth teased her about him.

'He's good company, but there's no chemistry,' she'd said with surety. She knew about chemistry. Once it had existed between her and Symon. Once.

The vicar frowned as he waited for a reply. 'If you've got a problem with Rod, we could find someone else.'

She blinked, collected her thoughts. 'Not at all, but you're such a fair chairman, Vicar, and it's likely to get sticky. Symon may come. Of course, if you aren't committed to the cause . . . '

His eyes twinkled. 'Of course we must help Ruth, but Marsh would be seen as more impartial than I would. We want everyone to attend, including the church people from the other side, but if I'm chairing it, they may stay away. You see my point, eh? I'm happy to call Rod and see if he's available, or an alternative would be for you to chair it.'

She laughed, shook her head. 'And you think I'd be seen as impartial. The mood I'm in, I wouldn't trust myself to run a balanced meeting. You're right, as usual, Rod would be ideal. Can I leave it to you to contact him?'

'I'll do it during the lunch break and

get back to you.'

As he showed her out, she asked, 'You and Mavis plan to be there?'

'Yes, my dear. The meeting has our blessing.'

Next, April visited each of the small properties she passed on her way back to Red Gum Track, and informed her neighbours of the arrangements. Yes, they were furious, they'd be there. Yes, they'd share the phoning around to notify as many locals as possible.

Having satisfied herself she'd talked to as many people as possible, she turned into her track jogging, operating again on adrenalin, as she planned the rest of her day, rehearsing what she'd say at the meeting. But she was unable to recall the light-hearted mood in which she'd set out this morning and her pace slowed. Basil spotted a rabbit and tugged with such strength that she dropped the lead and he sped off.

Her heart paused and then as suddenly began to pulse madly. Basil would come back. Symon had come back, and oh how she wished he hadn't. A couple of hours in The Hill and he'd turned her life upside down — again.

2

April's mind filled with tangled memories as she passed the back entrance to Symons Run. Once his family were spoken about in the district in the same deferential tones reserved for royalty. But times had changed and the ageing head of the third generation, Cyrus, had failed to produce a son.

His daughter, Cecily, was Symon's mother. Though he didn't carry the Symons family name, he was the old man's only living relative and everyone assumed him to be the heir.

Symon once told her with a touch of humour, 'Grandfather insisted I be christened Cyrus Symons Andrews. Apparently my father opposed it, but finally he and the old man compromised and agreed I'd be named Cyrus, but called Symon.'

She'd loved his smile, particularly

25

when it was directed at her, and she'd admired his unassuming nature. 'To me you've always been impressive,' she'd said, her eyes locking into his, turning his smile sensual, stirring her heart. 'So where were you christened? St Paul's Cathedral?'

'I hate talking about my family. It's boring.'

But it would take their minds off their feelings, ease the tension. 'The Symons' story is fascinating, Cyrus.' She'd forced a laugh.

Clearly he'd felt uneasy, too, for his laughter didn't carry its usual merry ring. 'You know it all, except, I always think I had a lucky escape.'

'But the name Cyrus has dignity, a history.' She'd kept the conversation light.

'Sure it has, but it sounds so pompous. My father did me a big favour by opposing the old boy over my name. In fact, it was the best thing he ever did for me.'

This time a laugh, an unconvincing

one, accompanied his words. Over the years of their friendship she'd observed that any reference to the father who'd died a year or two after Symon was born, always unsettled him, but she'd been unable to get him to open up on the subject.

More secrets. She wondered, as she stumbled over a rut in the road. When she almost lost her footing, it brought her back to today with a thud. Why in Heaven's name did she keep revisiting the past, when it was present which threatened to throw her hard-won control over her feelings for him into chaos.

She quickened her pace, anxious to leave The Run's entrance and the memories associated with it, behind. She had a meeting to plan.

Entering her home, she called, 'I'm back. Did you miss me, sweetness?' And hurrying through to the crudely built-in back veranda, she greeted little Jelly Bean.

She'd rescued the ringtail possum

from its mother's pouch when it was no more than the size and colour of a pink jelly bean. It scampered across the back of an old couch to her side, she brushed its soft, silky coat gently, curled its tail around her finger.

'Don't look at me with those big eyes, you are not getting anything to eat, I have a new baby to care for first.'

Jelly Bean was full of life, sticking its nose into everything, at home in every room of the house, and almost ready to leave. It sped off to a dark corner of the room.

Already April felt calmer. She splashed water over her heated face, poured herself a glass of chilled water from the fridge, and fell into a chair to drink it. But minutes later she roused herself. She had the baby to check on and feed.

Only yesterday a neighbour had rescued the young kangaroo from its dead mother's pouch and brought it to her to care for.

She hurried into the kitchen where she kept the ungainly little creature she'd christened Twiggy, because of its spindly back legs, in a pretend pouch fashioned from soft cloth. Tucked warmly into a child's multicoloured knitted jumper, the joey stared up at her with the softest, appealing brown eyes. She'd reared kangaroos from the joey stage before, and knew exactly what was required to give them a chance to live.

As she lifted Twiggy from her pouch she noted with pleasure the little one had started to grow hair. The really tiny, hairless joeys weighed only around a quarter of a pound, and had to be bottle fed every few hours, night and day. Their chances of survival were slight.

She always called the vet, Charles Bransgrove, first to check any animals she took in. He'd given Twiggy a cautious OK, and promised to call again when passing.

She tucked Twiggy into the crook of her arm, and though keyed up, she forced herself to hum a gentle tune as she prepared the tiny syringe of special milk. Sitting on the sofa, she took the phone off the hook, afraid if it rung it might frighten her small charge. Next, she set about coaxing the little creature with soothing words to suck from the syringe.

Joeys felt dislocated, missed the warmth and succour of their natural mothers. April learned this from experience. The feeding at this early stage of life required persuasion, patience, and today, with people to be contacted, plans to be made, it really tested her nerve. But Twiggy's large eyes spoke of helplessness, captured her heart, and the knot of anxiety in her stomach continued to ease as she settled to the task.

The joey started to suck slowly from the syringe, milk dribbled down the sides of its mouth. One day it too would be ready to leave. She hated saying goodbye to the orphan animal friends she rescued and reared, but uppermost in her mind lay the thought that they belonged to the Australian bush, not to her.

The animals were victims of bulldozers rampaging through their natural habitat in the name of progress and urban development. It forced them closer to the towns to find food.

Then she thought of Symon. Her heart did a double flip as she recalled the late afternoon they'd returned glowing and happy from lunch at a nearby winery. He'd placed his hands on her shoulders, she'd smiled up at him.

'Have I told you what your sensational smile does to me?' he'd asked.

'No, but I'm listening,' she'd murmured, her beating heart telling her this could be the moment when their relationship took a giant leap from best friend to forever and a day.

'I'm falling in love with you, April Showers.'

'Me, too,' she'd whispered.

They'd exchanged kisses on many occasions, seldom on the lips, always with affection and a hug. But this time it felt different, breathless, excited. This time his mouth found her lips and lingered there, arousing in her feelings she's never experienced before.

Her face burned now as she remembered how she'd considered vaguely resisting, but the joy of it swept her away, until Symon stepped back, tilted her chin with his index finger and said, 'I'm sorry, I was about to take advantage.' In a fog of confusion, she'd whispered, 'It wasn't all your fault.'

He'd crossed to a chair, stood behind it, as if afraid to be closer. 'I want you to be sure. I want us to be sure of our feelings. We don't come with the credentials for knowing what makes a happy marriage. My father married my mother for her money, and your parents . . . ' He'd displayed his hands. 'You've hinted often enough their marriage had nothing to recommend it.'

It made sense, but disappointed, she'd tried to smile as she'd flopped into a chair. 'I think I'm sure, but then

I'm older and wiser than you.'

'Older maybe, but I want you to know you're sure.'

She'd thought about pushing it and saying she was, absolutely, positively sure, but already the idea that it was he who had the doubts had settled in her head. And now it all came back to haunt her, to tease her. Had the few years difference in their ages influenced him? Why had he let her think he loved her?

At the time she'd said, 'Yes. We'll make sure together,' nodding her head, trying to appear definite. She'd suggested a cool drink so he wouldn't see the tears glistening in her eyes.

'You think I need to cool down?' he'd jested.

No, she thought, I don't want you to cool down, I want you to say you love me, to hold me, but she'd said lightly, 'You mightn't need one, but I do,' and escaped to the kitchen on legs which felt wobbly, and once there, reached for a tissue.

He'd stood at the kitchen door. 'I'll give you a hand.'

'I've got it covered.'

The tears were back in her eyes. One trickled down her cheek and fell upon little Twiggy. The joey jerked gently, bringing April back to the present. She sighed.

'Little one, here I am mooning about when I have things to do,' And tucking the joey back into the security and comfort of her pouch, she returned the bundle into its warm box by the kitchen range.

After recradling the phone, it rang almost immediately. Bob Daniels from Deep Valley Road was gung-ho about saving the post office.

'I don't care that it's young Andrews we're up against. Don't understand his motives, mind you, but he's spoiling for a fight if he thinks he can stroll back into town and start running things. The Symons mob no longer own the district. We're saving that post office, April. No sweat. It's part of our history.

We might even be able to restore it. leave it to me, love, to canvas the resident properties along my track and beyond for their support.'

April wondered if forming a small committee first might have been wiser than a full-blown protest meeting. After all she didn't have the details of Symon's takeover. When he appeared so unexpectedly . . . when she discovered it was he who threatened to rob them of their post office . . . well, she let her feelings cloud her judgement.

She shrugged. Too late to change things now. besides, nothing had really changed. Ruth needed the income from the post office. The locals needed the post office and someone as trusted as Ruth running it. If it moved to the store, Symons Hill would lose another business.

* * *

The coming protest meeting took on a life of its own. The phone kept ringing.

Symons Hill prepared to challenge Mr Andrews for its post office. Spurred on by support, April called the local paper. The editor agreed to send a reporter with a camera.

Gerry Hutter, a graphic artist who ran a small business from his holding, offered to do posters and a bundle of leaflets which he'd placed in strategic places around the shire.

By seven o'clock, April had worked out an agenda, faxed it to Rod, who'd agreed to chair the meeting, and organised the church ladies' auxiliary to arrange tea and biscuits afterwards.

Ruth also rang to say Symon had done a great job with the wire door, attaching new hinges, flywire and a latch. 'It's got a few more years left in it,' she added, obviously trying to sound cheerful.

'Bully for him,' April refused to let anything interfere with her antagonism towards him. She needed it to get her through the evening.

After feeding Twiggy again, settling

the mischievous Jelly Bean in her enclosure for the night, she made up a supply of milk for the next twenty four hours, biting into an apple as she worked.

It irked her that as she dressed for the meeting, she took care with her appearance, but darn it, she wanted Symon Andrews to see how well she'd been doing without him.

She slipped a red soft-wool roll neck jumper over her head, pulled on expensive well-cut slacks. Though it was not yet winter, church halls were notoriously cold. Finally she brushed out her pony tail, finger-combed her hair and examined the result in the bathroom mirror. Were there a few lines around her eyes?

'Of course not,' she told Basil, who followed her around the house, sensing she was preparing to go out, hopeful he might be, too.

Returning to the bedroom, she opened the wardrobe and glanced into the long mirror behind its door to get the full effect.

A voice in her head said, 'You've got real curves, April Showers.' Symon had told her. He'd laugh, as if embarrassed by the statement. Well, tonight he'd find that she still had those curves. But compelled to take a more honest look, she admitted they were no longer curves. She'd thinned down. Skinny, Ruth called her.

The farmlet and her artwork kept her on the move, and during extra busy periods, such as now when she had two native animals boarding with her, she didn't eat regular meals. Her animals always came before her own needs.

Finally, a glance at her watch told her she couldn't delay any longer. Stroking the sleeping Twiggy on her head, she said, a smile touching her lips, 'Don't go away little one. I'll be back soon.'

And shrugging into her black jacket, April located her flashlight, and prepared to set out on foot for the hall. Limited car parking space existed along the main road, so she'd decided to leave it for others who had farther to travel.

The rough track was deep in evening shadows, trees pulsated restlessly in the breeze. She loved the familiar sounds of the bush at night, the swish of an occasional bird on the wing, the rustle of a possum on night patrol. She trod the track with surety, her elastic-sided boots, smart and practical, cushioning its uneven surface.

Until . . . until she reached the back entrance to Symons Run, which had its sweeping drive in from the main road. There she faltered, her thoughts forsaking the coming meeting, inevitably winging to Symon and the past.

It was common knowledge among the old time locals that his mother, Cecily, had been forced to leave home after becoming engaged to marry a man unacceptable to her father.

Later, apparently forgiven, she'd returned with her husband, who died in a tractor accident a few years after Symon was born. He was raised at The Run under strict guardianship of his grandfather, the crusty old Cyrus.

The grandson was destined to inherit the property from Cyrus, for, after his mother died, he was the only direct descendant. Yet he had hastily departed the district as if he didn't care a toss about his family obligations.

In a small place like The Hill rumours had a way of travelling and of multiplying. For a month or two his sudden disappearance was debated with some heat as people gathered outside the post office after collecting their mail.

One maintained Symon had gone off to marry a young Melbourne socialite, another that he'd eloped with a model who wasn't welcome at The Run, a third that he'd lost a fortune at gambling and been cut off by his grandfather.

April had tried not to listen, but when Millie, the current housekeeper at The Run, finally confirmed that he had married, 'one of them city girls', she stopped snapping, 'What nonsense,' and shrugged when the locals said,

'History has a nasty habit of repeating itself, you know.'

But he had come back. Why? And where was his wife? Had she come with him?

Don't let the memories overwhelm you, she warned herself, trying to shrug off her malaise, you've got an important night ahead of you. Yet her thoughts ran on. Symon, the man she once respected as a person of warmth, integrity and principles, had almost certainly returned to The Hill to ingratiate himself with his ailing grandfather and secure his inheritance. It fitted with the actions of the man today, the one who was about to rob Ruth Henderson of her livelihood.

A shiver ran down her spine before she quickened her step, thankful to catch up with the Thorpes as they left their property which stood at the entrance to Red Gum Track.

'Super poster.' She laughed, nodding to their blue heeler dog, which carried a sign around its girth reading, *Symons Hill loves its Post Office*.

'Young Andrews is in for a mauling from the locals,' Greg Thorpe growled. 'If he thinks he can ride rough-shod over our little community his scheme will turn pear-shaped pretty quickly. We'll show him loud and clear the Symons family no longer have gentry status around these parts. You have to earn respect these days. You don't inherit it. Blood-oath, you don't.'

April nodded her agreement, but her heartbeat stuttered. The soppiest part of her, the part which would even find a commendable quality in a condemned killer, railed against seeing Symon publicly humiliated. These were his own people, she the outsider, born a city girl.

Her introduction to Symons Hill had come on school holidays which she spent with her mother on the small, rented acreage adjacent to Symons Run. When her mother died, surprisingly, for she had no idea she'd owned it, April received a solicitor's letter. Her mother had left her the farmlet.

Delighted, she'd abandoned her solitary life in a small, ugly suburban flat to make Symons Hill her home.

She straightened her shoulders. This wasn't the time to go soft. If people decided to trash Symon, he had only himself to blame. Her objective tonight was to see that Ruth Henderson retained the post office licence. She marched towards the hall, a determined tilt to her chin.

In the hall, Rod Marsh looked up from the table, where he sat on the small stage studying his agenda, and smiled. He appeared very confident, she thought, as she made her way forward. But when upbeat neighbours, some she didn't even know, greeted her, she too became confident — with a few hours' notice all these people had come to support Ruth.

The surge of adrenalin helped combat the unnerving thought that Symon sat somewhere in the hall. Watching her? Judging her? Disapproving of her?

Her glance ranged around the room,

seeking him out, steeling herself to make contact with those aloof blue eyes, to remind herself that he had stopped being on her side a few years ago, and her life no longer revolved around him.

Unable to locate Symon in the crowd of eager faces, she let out a long sigh of relief, and settled her attention on Ruth Henderson and her mother, Essie. They sat on the aisle of the front row.

Essie beamed, obviously enjoying the outing, the company, but the bad news Ruth had received clearly reflected on her face. She'd lost her gloss, the enthusiasm which usually radiated from her as she stood behind the post office counter. She returned April's encouraging smile and wave with a defeatist shrug of her shoulders.

Blast you, Symon, she thought, as she took her seat next to Rod, preparing to record the minutes of the meeting and action notes.

Rod placed his hand over hers,

smiled. 'You OK? You look a bit frazzled.'

He had green, sometimes grey, eyes, depending on the light and on the degree of his smile. Tonight they were green, thoughtful. He was thoughtful, practical, too, good company. They spent quality time together. And, as Ruth kept reminding her, he was eligible, mid-thirties with a fine reputation in teaching and administration, and he enjoyed living in The Hills.

'When are the Symon withdrawal symptoms going to disappear?' he occasionally asked in a jokey voice.

April would toss her head, laugh. 'Symon who?'

But her relationship with Rod still hadn't stretched beyond a kiss on the cheek when they said goodnight after a trip to the theatre. She always hurried away, confused about whether or not to encourage him, and in the solitariness of her bedroom she'd admit that once you've had a relationship packaged with magical strings and bows, second fiddle

45

didn't quite do it.

She gently withdrew her hand from Rod's. 'Thanks a bunch for the confidence boost. I did try hard not to look like a hag,' she said too brightly.

A man anxious to impress would have followed with a flow of flattery, but Rod was a teacher. 'Take a few deep breaths. You'll be fine.'

'I am fine. You don't have to worry.' She disliked herself for allowing his concern to irritate her.

'Good. If everyone's here, we'll start,' he responded in a business-like voice.

Everyone wasn't there. Still no sign of Symon. She mentally crossed her fingers. 'Go for it,' she said, but her heart was already pulsing out of control.

Rod tapped his pen against a glass to call the meeting to order, gave a short welcome, and asked people to sign the attendance register which was being circulated. Then he invited April to briefly outline the purpose of the meeting.

Taking a long breath as she stood up,

she tried to organise a look of confidence and competence, though her stomach hosted a battalion of butterflies. Hoping her hands, which held prepared notes, and her voice wouldn't reveal her inner turmoil, she launched into praise for Ruth's commitment to the district, her friendly, reliable service.

'Ruth's mother, Essie, who's also with us tonight, ran the post office before her, in the days when we could call her the postmistress,' she smiled, adding, 'and not feel we might be sued.' It drew applause, some hoots of laughter.

'If the post office closes we lose an important piece of Symons Hill history, the services of . . . ' And then came the sound of the door opening, a brief shuffling at the back of the hall. The thread of April's argument was lost.

She dared to raise her head beyond the crowd and for a heart-lurching instant her eyes locked into Symon's indifferent stare.

3

Symon stood just inside the door, tall, his golden-brown hair flopping, as it always did, across his forehead, a vaguely amused smile on his lips.

She placed the palms of her hands on the table to support herself, but it hampered her breathing.

' . . . the services,' she took a deep breath, straightened up, managed to continue, 'of a fine woman, a special person, one we all love and support in this town.'

'Here, here,' someone called.

She drew strength from the encouragement enabling her to finish her address with the strong message she'd prepared. 'We must not sit idly by and allow the post office to be stolen from us. We let the bank move out. We allowed our secondary school, the one many of you helped to finance at its beginning, to be amalgamated with our neighbouring school. The post office stays. I move that we set up a *Save the Symons Hill Post Office Committee.*'

To calls of agreement, foot stamping and clapping, April sat down. As she did, buoyed by the unarguable response, she ventured a second glance in Symon's direction, stayed focussed as she caught his attention. Raising her brows, she sent him a silent message. 'Sorry,' it said, 'this is one you won't win.'

The motion was seconded, then Ruth asked to speak. 'I appreciate your support. In fact I'm overwhelmed by it,' she said, her voice trembling with emotion, 'But I should point out that the post office building is in poor repair, and I can't afford to have work done on it. I understand why the postal authorities want to move it into the general store. There's liability insurance to think about, but if I lose my job . . . ' Tears gathered in her eyes.

Someone called, 'Shame.'

Another, 'We can't let Andrews get away with it.'

A tense, hostile moment followed as heads turned to the back of the hall, eyes to pinion him down.

Apparently unmoved, his deep, authoritative voice cut through the uncomfortable silence. 'Mr Chairman, as the new owner of the store, I'd like to speak against the motion.'

And without waiting for permission, he strode towards the front.

April's heart pounded. This was a new, tough, decisive Symon. The Symon she'd loved would have been conciliatory, have listened, weighed up the ideas before speaking. This new person was at least as handsome as the old one, and he looked intimidatingly impressive in a navy suit, white shirt and blue tie. And there, she decided with fleeting pleasure, he'd made a strategic error, for his business clothes projected an image of a successful city guy, an outsider. He'd have been wiser to come casual in a check shirt, moleskins and pretend he was one of them.

'I have to give him the floor,' Rod whispered to her. 'Can you cope?'

Impatient, she sighed. 'Of course I can. Give the man his moment. He's not going to change anyone's mind here.'

'Mr Andrews the meeting recognises you,' Rod announced.

Calls of, 'We don't want to hear you, mate,' and 'You've got nothin' to say that's going to impress us,' followed immediately.

'Please give Mr Andrews a Symons Hill fair go,' Rod pressed. 'You'll all have an opportunity to say your piece.'

'Thank you. Symons Hill is my home. It always will be. I was raised here,' Andrews began.

April narrowed her eyes. If he thought he could sway them with emotional talk like that he should think again. She sucked in her lips, quelling the impulse to interrupt and ask if the district was so important to him, why he'd deserted his home and his elderly grandfather; why he'd run from her without explanation.

But she'd played that emotional game in her mind far too often. The answer was always the same. There was no answer, and with his sudden return she'd discovered she still carried the scar of rejection. She still hurt.

'I'm speaking against the motion. This morning while I rehung the post office door, I took the opportunity to inspect the building on the off-chance that it could be saved and the community spared the upset of a lengthy and costly fight.'

'You don't own the building, mate,' someone called.

His smile held a suggestion of mockery. 'I don't think I said I owned it.' And refusing to be sidetracked, he went on, 'But in two weeks time I'll take over the post office operating licence, and knowing how important Ruth's building is historically, I assure you, I took an honest look at using it.'

He paused, placed his hands in his pockets, appeared even more comfortable.

'He's said enough, we're not interested in his lies,' came another shout.

Rod held up his hand for silence, as Symon continued. 'Frankly, to repair it would cost more than I'm prepared to risk. As a compromise, I'm happy to offer Ruth the job of running the post office from my store. I hope she'll think seriously about it, so we can forget this protest nonsense and pull together for the sake of the town. Personally I think you've been stirred up about nothing. I have great respect for Ruth and her competence. Leave us to settle this matter together.'

As he concluded his statement, he turned his gaze squarely upon April. Her fingers clutched tightly about her pen, but she tilted her chin, stared back at him, refusing to be drawn into an impetuous response.

One or two people clapped without enthusiasm. The gathering murmured uncertainly. Someone called, 'We can restore the post office ourselves with working bees, if it's all right with Ruth.' Applause and murmurs of approval followed.

'Mr Chairman, I think we should put the motion to the vote,' April prompted, afraid the meeting might get out of hand and start discussing other issues.

'Unless anyone else wishes to speak?' Rod suggested.

'Is Ruth going to accept Andrews' offer? No point us saving the post office if she is,' someone asked.

Ruth shook her head, stood up. 'I appreciate Symon's offer, but for personal reasons, I can't consider it.'

April knew why, as did the people closest to the Henderson family. But they remained tight-lipped, respecting Ruth's wish not to draw attention to the accelerating progress of Essie's Alzheimers, and her need of constant supervision.

If Ruth worked from the general store she couldn't have Essie by her side during the day.

'That's all I'm interested in,' Bob voiced. 'We save the post office for Ruth and old Essie.'

They voted for a committee. April stifled an urge to seek Symon out and indicate with raised brows and a confident tilt of her head that the result was never in doubt. She had no wish to have petty and churlish added to the list of faults he'd already listed against her.

With the committee formed, she agreed to become its note-taker and they scheduled a time tomorrow evening to meet at her home. As Rod declared the meeting closed and invited people to stay on for a cup of tea, she searched for Symon, but he had disappeared from the hall. Thank goodness she wouldn't have to face him again tonight. She mopped the sweat from her hands, stretched her legs and took a long breath.

Glancing at her watch, she decided she had time for a cup of tea before returning home to feed Twiggy. In fact her mouth was so dry she needed it.

Chatting, commenting on the victory, she made her way to the parish hall and joined the crowd milling around the table where the cups and urn were set out. But in the crush, she came face-to-face with Symon. Uncomfortable, confused, she stepped to one side, as he did, first to the left and then to the right.

He smiled. He still had an engaging smile when it reached into his blue eyes giving them a rich, royal softness. She'd fallen for that smile, foolishly romanticising he kept it only for her.

'It seems we can't avoid one another even when we try,' he said evenly. 'Let me get you a cup of tea. Still drinking it weak and black?'

He remembered. A bewildering wave of pleasure swept over her.

'Why yes.'

'Sit down. I'll bring it across.'

Why was he being so pleasant? Trying to influence her in some way? It wouldn't work. After all, she'd carried the night. And that affirmed, she decided she could afford to be pleasant in return. Besides, if he planned to resettle here, they couldn't go on ignoring or snubbing one another. 'Thank you, Symon. I'd appreciate that.'

As she made her way to a wall of empty chairs and dropped into one, she dragged in several refreshing breaths. Only now did she fully appreciate why Rod had been so solicitous. Her anxiety must have been obvious to those who knew how badly Symon had hurt her, and that would include a fair number of people gathered tonight.

Thank goodness she hadn't rushed off after the meeting, underscoring the impression she was still troubled by the broken romance. Of course that was nonsense.

But as Symon approached carrying two cups, she noticed with irritation how steady his hands were. Why wasn't he showing some disappointment or at least a shade of anger that he'd been rolled at the meeting. Ah, he'd loosened the knot of his tie, undone the top button of his shirt, that could suggest anxiety, she thought.

'I almost didn't make it tonight. I had to hot-foot it back from a business meeting in town.' He handed her a cup of tea.

She should have realised he was too savvy to have come to the meeting in business clothes without a good reason.

He took the chair beside her. His hip grazed her leg, she could feel his body warmth. Her cheeks hot, she gazed ahead, gripped the handle of her cup and dared to lift it to her lips for she needed a drink.

'These church halls don't get any warmer, do they?' he said.

'No.' She lied, for her body burned, her hands sweated around the handle of her cup.

'So, how are you?'

Polite conversation, but his eyes studied her, she dug deep for a sentence of more than one word. 'Fine, just fine.

Have you settled back at The Run?'

He nodded, dashed back hair from his forehead with his hand. How often had she reached up in the past, brushed it back for him with a smile, and been rewarded with a playful kiss.

'I've moved into the former gatekeeper's lodge. Grandfather's pretty low, so Millie suggested I come home. Not that he's made me very welcome, but I'm trying to please him. Physically, the poor old guy's only a shadow of himself, but he's still as sharp-tongued and as caustic as he always was. He's never really cared much about me.'

The almost reflective tone of his voice caught her attention. 'He probably finds it hard to show his feelings, Symon. I'm sure he loves you.'

'Maybe,' he said in an unconvincing voice.

'Who's idea was it for you to live in the gatekeeper's residence?'

'Mine. I don't want to be a burden on Millie. Old Cyrus is very demanding.'

'It's thoughtful of you. Millie's been wonderful. Your grandfather is lucky to have such a loyal and devoted housekeeper.'

'He's always been lucky with his housekeepers. Given a vote, I'd nominate your mother for the best housekeeper award at The Run, in any category.'

Startled, she turned to look at him and caught his smile, but it wasn't meant for her, it clearly happened as he thought of her mother, Jean.

'She was always so caring and kind.'

She frowned. As a child, she'd never found her mother particularly warm or caring. She'd loved her, of course, because kids naturally loved their mothers, but after Jean abandoned her husband and April while she was still in primary school, forgiveness didn't come easily. But it did happen.

'I don't think I knew her very well as a child, but after Mum took the job at Symons Run, and I spent the school holidays on the small farmlet, I found out how very fond she was of animals.

It helped me to understand her better, but I didn't realise you thought of her so . . . fondly.'

'It was boring at the big house when Jean wasn't around. My poor mother never got over losing my father so young. I'm told he was a bit of a ladies man and Grandfather only tolerated him because Mother adored him, and he wanted an heir. After Dad died in the accident, I remember trying to help Mother, cuddling up to her, trying to make her stop crying, but she always pushed me aside.'

How odd that they both felt — was it unloved or unwanted — by their mothers. Could that have been a intangible factor which drew them together?

In the past Symon had been reluctant to talk about his boyhood and she'd been sympathetic, for she hated recalling her own dysfunctional childhood. But now she listened intently to him. Being raised at The Run, she imagined, didn't equate with a child's view of fun and happiness.

'Why do you think that was?' she asked, the trying meeting forgotten.

'Poor mother, old Cyrus dominated her so. I think she forgot how to love after she lost my father so suddenly. Even if she'd had an opportunity to meet another man, she'd never have taken it. Grandfather gave her such a hard time over my father.' He paused, concern in his blue eyes. 'Good heavens, how on earth did I get into all this?'

She had no idea, but a smile came to her lips. 'Confession time?'

His face relaxed slightly. 'Forgive me. I haven't spoken of it as openly before. The Symons family isn't supposed to talk about their feelings. People are supposed to think everything at The Run is happiness and light.'

She gestured with her free hand. 'I'm flattered that you've confided in me. I'm a good listener if you feel the need to talk any more.'

He smiled slowly. 'I just want to assure you, your mum was a fabulous woman. She never allowed the old boy to dominate her — she knew exactly how to handle him. In the afternoons when she left the house, The Run reverted to being little better than a boarding house operating strictly on rules for this and that. When Jean was around it became a happy place. I thought the world of her.' He spread his hands, 'Confession over.'

'Don't apologise. I'm particularly interested in hearing how you felt about my mother. You didn't ever mention it before.'

'Really? I thought I had.'

She shook her head. 'I don't recall, but maybe I didn't want to hear it because I didn't find her very motherly.'

'Perhaps you didn't know her very well. I think she may have been lonely. You only came during the holidays . . . '

'I always came when she invited me.'

'You sound defensive. Did you ever think your father wouldn't let her have you? We often see things more clearly in hindsight.' His voice tapered off. He dragged his already loosened tie further apart. 'Is it hot in here or am I imagining it?'

She too felt uncomfortably warm. 'Perhaps it's all the hot air from the meeting.' Her attempt at humour pleased her, but she sped back to a more neutral subject, 'It seems I didn't know my mum very well. Of course, she was never unkind, and I loved spending the holidays up here. And I'm grateful to her for teaching me so much about caring for animals, but honestly, I always felt they meant more to her than I did.'

April turned her face up to him and smiled to let him know it no longer worried her. A light flashed before her eyes. The local paper reporter said from behind the residual glow of light from his camera. 'It'll make a nice picture, April — the opposing forces enjoy a very intimate chat after the protest meeting.' He laughed.

She groaned inwardly, annoyed with herself. She thought she had her life back on track ages ago. It had taken so little, his remembrance that she drank her tea weak and black, and she'd found herself communicating with him with the familiarity and ease of an earlier age.

Of course, she was no longer that person, he no longer had any influence over her, and yet . . . her memory bank kept homing in on the past . . . she'd almost forgotten how he'd duped her into believing he loved her. Even more maddening, he'd done it so easily, so skilfully.

Reacting with the speed of the camera flash, she jumped to her feet, hissed through clenched teeth, 'No you don't. It's not at all what I had in mind. I want the authorities to know we're an angry community, and Mr Andrews is to blame. We will not surrender our post office.'

The photographer signalled with the palm of his free hand. 'And muggins me thought you and Symon . . . well . . . that you were . . . ' He jerked his hand back and forth, mocked with his eyes, 'like that. Can I quote you?'

'Certainly, be my guest.' She turned accusing eyes upon Symon. 'Especially the bit about Mr Andrews trying to steal our post office.'

The cameraman grinned. 'If you ask nicely, I'll send you a copy of the happy snap for your mantelshelf. I didn't intend to use it.' He wandered off before she could respond.

Disposing of her cup on a spare chair, she watched him disappear, seething, and wishing she'd had time to tell him what to do with his photo, but that would only attract more attention.

'He was winding you up, April. You have a tendency to overreact,' Symon said, reminding her that he was the main cause of her grief.

'He had no right to take that shot.'

'You're not the even-tempered girl I used to know.'

She fixed her eyes on him. 'I wonder

why?' And with heat flushing across her cheeks, she immediately regretted her revealing response.

'OK, you're mad at me about the post office, but I didn't set out to upset Ruth or this town. I thought she'd jump at my offer to take the job at the store. She'd be well paid, more comfortable. I don't understand what's so personal that she has to refuse.'

'I don't think you understand a lot of things about people, Symon. And for the life of me I don't understand why you bought the store, anyway?' April tilted her head as she looked at him, but his attention was trained across the room. She tried to regain his attention. 'It's hardly your scene. You're an engineer by profession, heir to a wealthy landowner . . . '

'I thought I already said I came home to be with old Cyrus.'

'That only explains your presence here, not why you chose to buy the store, and take over the post office. It's not as if you need the money.'

'Perhaps the store needs my money.' He shuffled his feet, drank the last of his tea. 'It's similar to the post office, it requires a facelift. It's pretty run down. Someone's going to fall through those old arthritic floorboards one day.'

'Huh,' she tossed her head. 'I bet you think the whole town needs a facelift.'

'You certainly don't. You look wonderful, especially when your dark eyes spark with fire.' Then he displayed the palms of his hands, groaned, 'I've said the wrong thing again, haven't I?' He turned serious blue eyes upon her. He wasn't flattering her or jesting. His sincerity touched her heart.

'Excuse me?' she mumbled.

'I didn't intend to embarrass you.'

He'd noticed her burning cheeks and probably the uncomfortable way she flicked her hair back from her face. Come on, she urged herself, deal with it, think of a light-hearted reply.

'It's the kind of embarrassment I can handle,' she said, curving her lips, hoping the smile would reach her eyes.

The man wasn't a monster. Of course he wasn't. Nor was he the person she thought he was. She simply had to live with that.

And, as if to rescue her from further uneasiness, a shriek came from across the room. Ruth was surrounded by people when April reached her.

'It's mother,' she cried, 'she's disappeared. I should have kept an eye on her. She must have wandered off while I was talking to Rod.'

Greg Thorpe patted Ruth on the shoulder. 'Don't panic, she can't have gone far. We'll find her.'

'But it's so dark out here. I was only distracted for a minute or two and . . .' Ruth's hand shot to her head in a gesture of anger and frustration.

Greg put his arm around her. 'Don't go blaming yourself, love. We'll spread out, search the area. Let's go, fellas.'

Symon stood on the edge of the group, his voice firm and strong. 'I suggest we dispense with the gang mentality and do this in an organised way. Where is she most likely to go, Ruth? Home? The picnic ground? A friend's place?'

Ruth shook her head. 'Anywhere. That's the problem. She doesn't have a destination, she just wanders off.'

'OK, Rod. Can you allocate teams to search different areas? Make sure each one has a mobile phone and a flashlight.'

'Good idea. We can check in every fifteen minutes. We'll find Essie,' Rod responded, already jotting down areas and allocating searchers.

Everyone nodded their approval at Symon's decisiveness, his ability to take the panic out of the situation. He may have lost favour this evening, but right now he was in the process of regaining respect.

Rod instructed the people to various search areas before turning to Symon, who'd returned from his car with a map of the area. 'Here's the list, Andrews. I've rostered you to stick around at the hall. Groups will check in with you every fifteen minutes.'

And turning to April, who stood to one side, he said, 'We'll take the main road as far as Red Gum Track, and then along your road as far as your home.'

Before she could move to Rod's side Symon intervened. 'That track's familiar to me. April and I know every eucalyptus, every bush. I've got a better suggestion. You're not a local, Rod, wouldn't it make more sense for you to hang around here and co-ordinate? You seem very good at that.'

He crossed to stand by April, addressed her as if it were already settled. 'We'll search as far down the track as it goes.'

He already had his arm at her elbow. 'You agree, don't you, April? If Essie's gone down our track we're the best bet to find her.'

He'd called it 'our' track, and once it had been. But not any more. Dare she risk going with him, retracing their earlier footsteps? Would the shadow of the past interfere with the purpose that

71

had brought them together? It might, and she thought it unwise to risk it.

'I'm not so sure,' she replied.

'What's your problem?' Symon demanded.

'I have to get home to the animals,' she muttered.

Impatience glittered in his eyes. 'We're going in your direction. It won't delay you.'

'It's up to you, April. Andrews and I can co-ordinate if you'd prefer to, but you're not going to get home to those animals.'

Rod, she suspected, knew exactly why she vacillated and had offered her an out.

She swept her hair back from her face. 'Sorry, I'm wasting everyone's time. Thanks, Rod, but Symon's right. We know the track . . . '

4

April hurried ahead in the gleam of Symon's flashlight, her shadow casting a ghostly, mocking shape ahead of her. She'd trodden Red Gum Track with Symon in the days when she thought he loved her, but she'd closed the door on all those memories. The important thing was to find dear old Essie before she came to any harm.

Symon caught up with her along the main road, strode ahead, grumbling, 'Isn't this just what we needed. I've had a rotten day. Now this. What the devil could the old girl be thinking of going walkabout without telling anyone? If Ruth and her mum are putting on an act hoping to draw more sympathy, it's not going to . . . '

'Ruth and Essie? How could you even think it?'

'Some old people have a knack of

getting their own way. You're looking at an expert on the subject. Grandfather has turning things to his advantage down to an art form. He plays on the fact that everyone will overlook his rudeness and selfishness and do his bidding because he's old.'

His bitter tone surprised her, triggered a chord of interest. 'You sound as if you feel you were trapped into coming home?' she ventured, hoping to draw him out.

'I didn't say that.'

'You inferred it. Your new found wisdom on our senior citizens comes from spending a few years in corporate life, I suppose? And you have the audacity to accuse old people of being selfish,' she snapped.

'I've lived most of my life in my grandfather's house, under my grandfather's rules and influence. Not any more. Don't expect me to apologise for being realistic. Realism — that's what the corporate world has taught me.'

She understood the new Symon a little better, but it didn't mean she liked him or excused his mean-spirited outbursts.

'No-one's asking you to apologise, but don't expect me to feel anything but scorn for the egocentric person you've become.' April dragged in her breath. She didn't quite believe her own rhetoric, especially when she'd glimpsed the old Symon back at the hall when he'd tempered his remarks with thoughtfulness and kindness.

She stumbled on a stone, uttered a small cry, but regained her footing without reaching out to him. 'Would you mind walking a little slower and shining the torch on to the ground so I can see where I'm going.'

'Take my hand.'

'Forget it.' She edged away from him, tried to concentrate on what they were supposed to be doing, and called Essie's name into the darkness.

'April, we're on the same side at the moment. Is it too much to expect you to suspend your contempt for me until we find Essie?'

'So you've changed your mind. You don't think we're wasting our time any more?'

'I still reckon we'll find Essie tucked up warm and snug in bed. And here we are stumbling around in the cold.'

'Poor old Symon,' she patronised. 'He's cold. Care to borrow my jacket? It's woollen and lined.'

'If you're hinting for me to hand over mine to you, why don't you just ask?'

'I wouldn't accept it even if you did the gentlemanly thing and offered it. You're carrying on like a spoilt brat.'

'I seem to recall back at the hall, you mentioned you were anxious to get home. Well, so are we all. So let's concentrate on why we're here,' he growled.

They'd reached Red Gum Track. Without street lighting, it felt as if they were turning into a long dark tunnel, for giant eucalyptus bent by the north winds met overhead, allowing only the occasional hint of moonlight to penetrate. The breeze whispered through the branches as unnerving shadowy shapes formed. But this was April's track. And his, she thought, her heart leaping. They'd celebrated it together. Shared it on their morning jobs, their evening strolls. Was he remembering now, as she was? She soon had her answer.

'So how about it? I'll bet you a cup of coffee Essie's back home.'

Her scratchy mood returned. 'We'd have heard on the mobile. Symon, I think it's time you knew the truth about Essie. Ruth doesn't want it generally known, but for obvious reasons I'm making an exception in your case.'

'Don't feel obliged.'

She ignored his cynicism. 'Essie suffers with Alzheimer's disease. She can't be left alone for any length of time because she wanders off. In the post office, Ruthie can keep a constant eye on her mother.'

'She'll only be next door to the store.'

April sighed, raised her voice impatiently, sending an animal lurking in nearby bushes scurrying into action. 'For goodness sake, didn't you hear what I said? She wanders off, literally. Think about it. Would you allow Essie to sit by Ruth in your store all day? Of course you wouldn't. It would be bad for business, you'd argue.'

'I'd have to think about it,' he said slowly. 'She's in the habit of wandering off, you say?'

'Yes. It's part of the condition. In the post office Ruth can keep track of her, and Essie enjoys the contact with the customers, people she's known all her life. Can you see now why Ruth can't accept your offer?'

He reached out. Alarmed, she felt his hands grip her shoulders, bite into her jacket as he swung her around. For the smallest breathtaking second she wondered if he was about to kiss her, and her body tensed. To resist, of course.

But his voice cut through the darkness. 'April, why the devil didn't you or Ruth tell me all this instead of tipping a very public bucket on me, treating me as if I'm a monster. I'm not impressed.'

She wrenched herself free, hurried on, talking at the same time. 'Ruth didn't want it to be public knowledge yet, and whether you're impressed or not doesn't carry the slightest weight with me. I'm concerned only with making sure Ruth and Essie have a comfortable future.'

He made up the ground between them. 'It's almost as if you wanted me to antagonise the town. I was entitled to know.'

'Ruth didn't think so or she'd have told you herself.'

'OK, so you're not entirely to blame.' His voice tapered off.

'Not entirely?' she mocked. 'Oh, come on. I was honouring my promise to a good friend.'

'But not any more because it suits you. If you'd suggested Ruth confide in me instead of calling out the cavalry, we could have had a calm discussion, and probably been able to negotiate a satisfactory outcome. As it is I'm public enemy number one in my own town.'

He sounded upset, or was it disappointed? It touched a chord of guilt within her. His sudden arrival in town had clearly thrown her, yet the need to defend herself prevailed. 'I can't see how it changes anything. You secretly bought the post office licence and Ruth's out of a job in two weeks' time.'

'It makes a difference. I know you won't believe this, but I care about the people of Symons Hill.'

'Hah, I suppose that's why you left in a cloud of dust.' She couldn't keep the contempt from her voice.

He ignored her sarcasm and stormed ahead shining the light beam into the thicket beyond the track, calling Essie's name. But April guessed it had more to do with distancing himself from her and her accusations.

The night seemed to close about her, threatening her. She shivered and hurried to catch up to him, stumbled a couple of times, but was soon by his side. 'Look, I'm sorry if you feel I misled you.'

He pushed on, silent. Could he be thinking about returning the licence to Ruth?

As they reached the gate on to her property, she prompted, 'At the risk of upsetting you again, now that you have the facts, will you change your mind about the post office?'

His breath materialised in the crisp air. 'If only it were that simple. After I bought the store, the postal authorities approached me to take over their business. Ruth's place is a designated hazardous public place. I would have thought that pretty obvious, but I seem to be the only person who's noticed. April, I've never thought of you as a person with a closed mind.'

'Me either,' she bit back.

Swinging open the gate with unnecessary vigour, he stepped back for her to pass through. As they climbed the long, winding slope towards the house, every now and then the uneasy silence between them was disturbed by a rustling in the trees.

He directed the light into the bushes, but from familiarity they both knew it came from a native animal on the prowl. Unscripted, they took it in turns to call Essie's name, but as if written into the play, they ignored one another.

Which left April wrestling with confused thoughts. Had she been unfair to him, closed her mind to him because of their past? Finally, unable to face her doubts in the dark, cheerless silence, she tried to cut through the tension with an unprovocative question. 'You said earlier you have plans to do up the store? I suppose you intend to put in a manager?'

'I'll run it myself. The present owners are struggling to make a living. I intend to turn that around and make the business profitable.'

She couldn't control her taunting tone when she replied, 'I wouldn't expect anything less. You are a Symons.'

'If not by name, then by breeding, eh?'

'I couldn't have said it better myself.'

'Ever thought it can be a disadvantage? People brand me a Symons, their opinions of me are coloured by it, they judge me by it.'

April felt a wave of conscience. 'If that's what I was doing, my apology.'

He tilted his head. 'Accepted. April, can we return to discussing the post office without getting heated? Have you taken a good, hard look at the building? It's falling down. It's an eyesore in the town.'

'I go in there every day.' She felt inclined to snap at him, but reminded herself to stay cool.

'People can become used to things they see every day.'

'I guess, but Ruth doesn't have the money to do it up, and that's something I can't get used to.'

'As usual you're worrying about things you can't fix. And your protest has come far too late. Tonight everyone said they cared, but you've waited until now to act.'

'You were here for a lot of the time,' she charged, 'how come you didn't see it coming?'

'You're losing it again.'

'Because I care about people.'

'I had other things on my mind. Now I'm trying to solve the problem in a constructive way, looking for compromises.'

'Me too. We simply have to do something to help Ruth.'

'Yeah. Which puts us on the same team.'

They had almost reached the house when he flashed the beam into nearby trees in response to a sound. It caught the luminous eyes of a possum. She glanced at Symon and in the darkness, his eyes seemed to glow too. City life hasn't taken the country out of the boy after all, she thought, a well of pleasure surging in her.

She smiled up at him, but as he

lowered the flashlight, she noted the glow had already left his eyes.

Disappointment ate into her already unsettled mood. He'd been moved so fleetingly by the memories of wandering the bushland at night, spotlighting for possums, koalas and kangaroos.

When she left home this evening, she had turned the veranda light on. As they approached the steps, it caught him in silhouette as he raised his shoulders. 'Perhaps we can do both — save the building and help Ruth.'

'We, as in you and the community?' Her tone reflected her disbelief.

'Sure. I'm attached to the old building. Perhaps you aren't aware of the romantic yarn about my great grandfather?'

A surge of interest made her pause. 'Sounds intriguing, do tell.'

'Great grandpappy set up a Miss Mason as the original . . . er, is it okay to say postmistress?'

'Get on with the story,' she said lightly.

'Folklore has it he fell desperately in love with the said Miss Mason but, as the daughter of a farm labourer on Symons Run, she wasn't considered suitable for the heir.'

Suitable? April clenched and unclenched her hands. She had long believed snobbery still ruled in the Symons family. Sometimes, she thought, that old Cyrus really believed he and his family were superior people. It could be the missing link. It could explain why Symon left town so suddenly.

As the daughter of a former house-keeper at The Run, the old man would never have consented to his only grandson and heir marrying her. It hurt like the devil to accept this could be the case.

She desperately didn't want to even vaguely consider that Symon had allowed his grandfather to bundle him off to the city to seek out a socially acceptable wife. But there were moments of weakness when the ugly thought that he had put his quest to secure his inheritance before everything else slipped into her mind, mocking her. A cold shiver ran up her spine. She dismissed it with a determined tilt of her chin.

'So what's new?' she asked bluntly.

'You're thinking of my mother and father?' He turned away, dragging at his loosened tie.

'Actually, I was thinking of you. Did your grandfather approve of the woman you married?'

She immediately regretted her probing question, for she didn't really want to hear the answer. Without waiting for his reply, she stumbled up the steps of the veranda and pushed open the door.

Basil bounded up the hall, his tail swishing a greeting. Patting him, talking to him, her nervous tension eased as the familiarity of the house reassured and calmed her. Twiggy waited to be fed, and the thought of her baby 'roo lifted the heaviness from her heart.

He followed her, his voice strangely

husky. 'It doesn't look as if Essie came this way. If it's OK with you, I'll phone back to the hall in here where it's light.'

But his nearness threw her immediately. He seemed to hem her in, drawing the walls around her, closing off her chances of escape from her confusing emotions. The walk home, the search, the shadows created by an insignificant moon, had all offered protection, a cloak of concealment, hidden from him her body language and the pain and uncertainty in her eyes.

She said quickly, 'Please go. I'll let them know we've drawn a blank.'

'I want to talk to Marsh myself in case there've been any developments. It looks as if the old lady hasn't been found or we'd have heard. There may be something more I can do tonight. I plan to go back to the hall to see what the state of play is.'

She strode down the hallway, heard him breathing close by her, searched for conversation to drown out the beat of her heart.

'I'm afraid I can't do any more tonight. Twiggy will be waiting for a bottle.'

'Twiggy?'

He didn't sound all that interested, but she explained anyway, glad to transfer her thoughts from him to the 'roo. 'Didn't I mention my baby?'

He stopped short, ran both hands through his hair. 'Excuse me? You have a baby?'

April guessed what he thought and a smile came to her lips. 'Yes, a joey. It was rescued from its dead mother's pouch a few days ago and brought to me to nurse.'

'Ah,' he said on a long sigh.

A crooning sound came from the kitchen area. April stiffened, stood still, placed her finger to her mouth to indicate silence. A wailing sound came again.

'Did you hear that? What on earth can it be?' she whispered.

'Maybe you left the radio on?'

She shook her head. 'No.'

'The joey doing a jig?' he suggested with a grin.

She smiled spontaneously. 'She's too small to get out of her pouch. And it's not Jelly Bean. I put her to bed before I left. Someone's in there.' April crept towards the kitchen, Symon's hushed steps at her back. At the door, she stopped suddenly.

Symon almost cannoned into her. She turned her lovely laughing eyes up to him. For an impulsive moment his arms reached out to her, but they fell helplessly to his side. He didn't have the right to hold her.

'Can you beat that,' she whispered, pointing towards the kitchen.

Beyond her he saw a figure sitting in a rocking chair nursing something in her lap. A woman? A quivery off-key voice singing, 'There'll be blue birds over . . . ' floated towards them.

'Shush,' April cautioned, dragging Basil back by the collar, blocking Symon's progress. 'Let's watch for a while. It's lovely isn't it?'

'Lovely,' he repeated, his gaze on April. She looked quite beautiful, vibrant, her face aglow in the half-light of the hall.

He took a backward step. 'What on earth's going on in there?'

'It's Essie. We've found Essie.'

Essie started a second verse of her song, obviously unaware of their presence. He bristled with impatience to get out of here, and said quite loudly, 'I should ring Marsh and let him know we've found her. I assume I can tell them she's fine?'

'I'm sure she is. Tell Ruth I'll bring her home after she's fed Twiggy.'

'Let me take her back. You've had a very busy time tonight.'

She shrugged tired shoulders. 'Whatever. Turn on the light and make the call from here. I don't want to alarm Essie.'

As she walked away her fragrance went with her. He made the phone call, all the time watching April through the doorway as she approached the old lady. Her hair awry, Essie looked very confused until the younger woman reached out, brushed her hand over Essie's cheek, spoke softly. 'Essie, it's April. It's time to feed Twiggy. Would you like to do it?'

Essie's face crinkled into a smile. 'Can I?'

The old lady rocked back and forward, hummed, as April took the prepared milk formula from the fridge, transferred some into a syringe and warmed it under the hot tap. Arranging the joey comfortably into Essie's lap, she placed the syringe into Twiggy's mouth and wrapped Essie's hand around it. The baby 'roo protested briefly, before nestling back into her lap and sucking.

'She's my baby. Isn't she sweet?' Essie smiled down at her charge, as Symon entered the room quietly, anxious not to disturb her.

The joey, he thought, was anything but sweet with its spindly back legs, peaked ears and scantily covered flesh.

In fact baby 'roos had very little going for them in the looks department, but they had appealing eyes and an irresistible vulnerability.

April had always loved helpless animals. It hadn't surprised him when she gave up her city secretarial position and moved to Jean's farmlet after her mother died and left her the acreage. What had surprised him was that Jean had owned the farmlet which he always believed was part of the Symons Run estate.

'Essie, do you like her name? I called her Twiggy?' April said, leaning from her chair and stroking the joey's head.

'Who are you? You don't know her name,' Essie said querulously. 'I called her Mary after my mother.'

'I'm sorry, Essie. I'm April. We often talk in the post office and you and Ruth come to visit.' She smiled gently.

'Then you should know the baby's name is Mary.'

'Mary's a lovely name, but don't you think she looks like a bundle of twigs with big eyes and a tail?'

Twiggy's mouth remained clamped around the teat.

Essie dropped her hand away and started to stand up, Basil barked.

'I'm taking Mary home, she wants to go home. it's too noisy here.'

Symon stepped forward. 'Not for a while yet, Essie. The baby's still got a nasty cold and it's chilly outside. Better to leave her here where it's warm for a few more days. But I'm sure Doctor Stewart will be happy for you to visit when you want.'

April raised her brows, obviously amused at her promotion to 'doctor'. 'Of course you can, Essie. I'll come and get you. you mustn't walk all this way on your own again.'

Suddenly, as if she'd lost interest in the joey, Essie thrust Twiggy into April's arms. 'I'd better go home. Mother will think I've missed the train. I'll get into trouble.' She smiled like a mischievous child.

'It's OK,' Symon intervened. 'She knows where you are. She's coming by to fetch you in the car. April, would you like me to walk her down to the gate to meet Ruth?' Symon suggested.

'I'd appreciate that. I need to finish feeding Twiggy. You'll find a warm coat on the hall stand. Put it around her shoulders. And don't let her out of your sight. If she wanders off again . . . ' she whispered.

Basil's tail wagged. He bounded up to Symon. 'Sorry, mate, you can't come. You're first duty is to protect your mistress.'

April laughed briefly. 'Goodnight, and thanks, Symon. We'll talk later about Ruth's problem.'

Symon intended to come back once he'd safely delivered Essie to her daughter. He couldn't ignore the dark smudges under April's eyes. She looked spent by the events of the day. If he could help in some way, settle the 'roo, make her a snack, he wouldn't take no for an answer.

He'd risk irritating her and return to the house.

5

When the doorbell sounded, April sighed, got up still cuddling Twiggy and, in no mood for more visitors, called testily, 'It's too late to open the door. Come back tomorrow.'

The commotion roused Basil from the mat and, belatedly, he raced towards the entrance, barking to signal to the late night visitor that he was on guard duty.

But the door swung open as he reached it and April heard Symon drawl in a skittish tone, 'I'm back.' She hurried into the passage, unsure whether to feel relieved or annoyed. But as Basil jumped up on Symon, greeting him as if family, annoyance won out. She'd often tried to explain to her effervescent pooch that Symon had become persona non grata in their home, but once a labrador bonded to someone . . .

'Traitor,' she whispered to him, 'you

need some fresh air,' and she stood aside to let him out.

Symon stepped uncertainly into the hallway leading to the sitting room.

'I thought I suggested you go home.'

She glared at him, wiped Twiggy's dribbly mouth with a tissue from her pocket.

'I decided to come back to see if I could help in any way, and to give you some advice.'

Returning to the kitchen, she addressed him over her shoulder, 'No more advice tonight, please. I'm all advised out.' And stifling a yawn, added, 'How did Ruth greet Essie?'

'Hugs and tut-tuts, naturally. She said to say thanks. She'll catch up tomorrow.'

April made the joey comfortable in her pouch, stroking her head. 'You're going to grow big and strong, aren't you, Twiggy?' She turned back to Symon. 'She looked so vulnerable when I first saw her.'

'Essie or the 'roo?'

She smiled gently. 'Both, of course, silly. Thank goodness Twiggy's drinking now.'

'You shouldn't leave your house open so people can wander in. You could walk in and find a thief . . . I don't want to frighten you, but . . . '

'I'm not frightened in the least. The Hill doesn't attract a criminal element.'

'That's naïve and I think you know it.'

'I've got Basil here to protect me, you know.'

He laughed. 'I could stroll in here any time and rob you blind. Basil would probably help me.'

She tried not to smile, gave a throwaway reply. 'But why would you? I haven't got anything you want.'

Her hand shot to her mouth to hold back her gasp. She hadn't meant it the way it sounded. In the strained silence which followed, she moved behind the sofa, wondering with a knotted stomach how he'd interpret her words.

She had her answer immediately for he raked hair back from his face revealing beads of perspiration. He'd misconstrued her statement in the most embarrassing way and thank goodness he left it alone, for he could feel no more awkward than she did herself.

'Rod Marsh seems a nice guy. Good principal?' he asked, flourishing his hands. Why did she have to notice how long and tender they looked, as if they hadn't seen hard work in a year or two? Once he had laboured on the orchard attached to The Run with a vigour and enthusiasm to match any of the outdoor employees, and his hands had become toughened, tanned.

The time to ask him to leave and insist upon it had long since expired, so why didn't she simply turn her back on him and go to bed?

'Excellent,' she said.

'Are you two an item?'

'We're very good friends,' she emphasised the very.

'I'm pleased for you. He seems to have everything a girl could want.

Women probably think he's a good looker, he's got a steady job, he's about the right age and . . . '

She cut in. 'You could add, he's considerate, caring, open and doesn't put women down? They're the qualities I look for in a man.'

'I was about to say he seems smitten. I've noticed the way he looks at you.'

'It's none of your business, Symon,' she said, removing her jacket, draping it over a chair, finger-combing her hair. 'So, if you'll excuse me, I'm desperate for sleep. Twiggy has to be fed again in four hours.'

'Four hours?' His voice rose. 'How can you survive with so little sleep?'

'I've managed so far without your approval.' The tilt of her head, her eyes mocked him.

She hurried to the kitchen where she rinsed the joey's bottle under the tap, and left it to drain, conscious with every move that Symon lingered close by. Sighing, she turned to face him, and said with determination, 'Time to go,

Symon. Goodnight for the first and last time.'

Symon didn't quite understand what kept him there, but it had something to do with being back in this comfortable and familiar sitting room with her. His glance ranged around it as he searched for a reason to stay and noticed for the first time an artist's easel stood by the window looking out on the back garden. It aroused his interest, drew him across to it to take a closer look. A watercolour of a pair of delicate fairy wrens was in progress.

'Your work?'

'Yes.'

'It's wonderful, April. Exquisite detail and colour.'

The tiredness lifted from her voice. 'I'm glad you think so. It's my major source of income these days. People like my work, and I can paint at home and care for my animals at the same time.'

'Not unlike Ruth and her mother. I suppose that's why you understand her plight.'

'Anyone with a heart would understand it.'

She didn't hold back, left him in no doubt how she felt about him, yet he tilted his head, asked, 'And you don't think I've got a heart?'

'You said it.' Her voice again became unyielding, her stance stiffened. He had the feeling he'd taken a blow to the solar plexus.

He'd been an optimist of inflated proportions to hope she'd react any differently, yet he couldn't forget how loving and caring she'd been in the past, and he found it difficult to bury a hope that they could again be friends.

'Ouch,' he said, trying to make light of her retort. 'But, April, I know a work of art when I see it. I'd like to buy a couple of your paintings to hang in the lodge.'

'I have a waiting list of people wanting to buy. I take orders at art shows.' She sounded smug, but why wouldn't she? The paintings would have wide appeal.

'Put me on the list. I expect to be around for some time.' And anxious to ease the tension, he suggested, 'Before I go, at least let me make you a cup of tea?'

She shook her dark hair. It shone in the light as it swished across her shoulders. She had always worn it long — a dark, glossy mirror capturing and reflecting the light. He'd noticed it at their first meeting. His mind drifted back to that sunny afternoon.

He'd climbed the farm fence between Jean's acres and Symons Run to recover a football, believing no-one was around. But, she'd shot from behind a tree, almost as if she'd been watching, waiting for him to encroach on to her turf.

And kicking the football farther into her territory, she swished back her dark hair, put her hands on her hips and said impertinently, 'This is Gumbooya — my mum's place. Boys aren't allowed here.'

She was taller than he, perhaps two or three years older — superior, bossy, a typical girl. But he'd decided not to ruffle her up too much in case she turned out to be like most girls — a cry baby. He'd already noted now skilfully girls used their tears to get their own way.

'Who cares. You're only a stupid girl, anyway. I'll get my football and leave,' he'd said, moving forward to collect it.

He'd made his first mistake with her. She'd fronted him, her slight build unchallenging, but her height and glare halting him. 'Did you think to ask? You're trespassing.'

He'd tried to stand tall. 'So, I didn't ask. And it's trespassing. What are you going to do about it?' He'd pushed by her and collecting the ball made a dash for the dividing fence. There, in safety, he paused.

'It's a stupid little property anyway, and it's got a stupid name.'

As he'd climbed back into home territory, she'd yelled, 'Hey, you, little boy,' and as he'd swung around, she'd added, 'It's aboriginal for 'resting place'. It's not named after someone's old grandfather, so there.'

She'd poked out her tongue at him, placed her hands back on her hips and said, 'Good riddance. And don't come back again, Simple Symon Andrews. You scare the animals.'

He'd laughed, mostly because it pleased him that the snappy girl knew who he was. But unknown to his mother, he'd started checking with Jean whether 'that girl' was staying with her for the holidays, and finding excuses for secret visits.

Together, during holidays they'd forged an uneasy alliance. He'd begun to call her April Showers just to hear her unleash a string of unladylike words.

She'd responded by calling him Simple Symon when she chose. Later he'd persuaded her to cut it down to S.S. and secretly they'd called one another A.S. and S.S.

From the beginning, she'd at once amused and filled him with awe. Boys he was used to. Girls were the world's great mystery.

This one wasn't like the sisters of his school friends or the girl cousins he had. She could match and sometimes better things he did.

She dared to climb trees, to steal fruit from the orchard. She'd taught him to milk Jean's cow, to bury the dead and repair the fencing after the fox raided the hen house, and to track a small family of kangaroos. They'd built a bird hide.

Unknown to anyone at the big house, he'd climb from his window on warm nights and they went spotlighting for the bushland's night wanderers.

His mother used to hug and kiss him when he came home from boarding school vacations looking excited and happy.

She hadn't realised his excitement mostly stemmed from the anticipations of spending time with A.S.

'Hello.' Her voice cut through a fog of memories. The kettle had filled, water poured over the lid.

'I said no to tea,' she said crisply, 'but by all means, have one yourself.'

He shrugged, vaguely still cloaked in memories.

There was so much he wished to tell her, so much he longed to say to her, so much that must remain unsaid.

'Why don't I stick around, doze on the old sofa? If I set the alarm, I can feed Twiggy. You go off to bed.'

He saw the surprise, the questioning in her dark eyes, but also read her determination in the tilt of her head.

'Thank you, but it's my job, my commitment. You have your store. I have my animals. I'm going to bed for the next four hours. Please yourself what you do, but don't interfere with my routine.'

She checked out Twiggy, opened the back door and called Basil in. After patting and hugging the dog, she turned back to Symon. 'You're still here?'

'And you still don't want any help?'

107

'That's what I thought I said.'

He detected only weariness in her voice. It had always been an improbable dream that he could return to The Hill and expect to befriend her. Their relationship had journeyed too far for that to be a realistic ask. He'd hurt her. She resented him. End of story.

The thought of being powerless to change anything knotted his insides. If only he could have ignored his grandfather's illness and stayed away.

He raked hair back from his forehead, ran his fingers over beads of sweat which had formed there. Why torment himself going over it again and again? There was no quick fix. No fix at all.

He sighed. 'If you're sure I can't help, I'll be on my way. I guess we'll run into one another from time to time.'

She paused in the doorway. 'We can't avoid it, but Symon's Hill is big enough for two adult people.' With an unconvincing smile, she stalked from the room.

'I'll call by sometime,' he suggested,

to the empty walls, knowing that calling by wasn't an option. A gut wrenching sense of loneliness, even more desolate than the one he'd had when he walked out on her last time, flooded over him.

As he closed the back door and strolled into the night, he knew for certain any hope of friendship with her had been a fool's dream. The next time he saw her he'd make sure he treated her as if she were no more than an old acquaintance.

★   ★   ★

April rose early, lazily prepared breakfast, tried to concentrate on the radio news, but everywhere there were reminders of Symon — at her easel, at the sink, by the sofa, she heard his beautifully modulated voice. She sniffled. Was that his aftershave?

Seizing up a deodorising spray can, she thumbed the nozzle, and mist gently cloaked the room, leaving an odour of lavender. She felt better for the emotional energy she'd spent, too. And when Basil came to her with the leash in his mouth, his tail wagging, she resolved not to let Symon's reappearance in town interfere with her resolution to resume her morning jog.

After taking a peep at Twiggy and Jelly Bean to make sure they were safe and comfortable, they set off down the driveway at a gentle gait.

Mildly stiff from the effort yesterday, April built gradually into a steady stride. The wind teased at her pony tail, the morning sun filtered through the trees. As usual, Basil set the early pace.

Her sense of freedom, positive thoughts, returned, as yesterday's troubles faded in significance. As a community they would find an answer to Ruth's problems. And at twenty-nine, she possessed the maturity to deal with Symon's presence in The Hill. She'd served her apprenticeship in grieving.

As if to undermine her purpose, as the track angled back on itself, Symon emerged from the rear entrance to The Run wearing a singlet, shorts and trainers. Her steps faltered, her heart raced. She hadn't expected to see him, hadn't prepared for it, and it was too late to turn back.

Somehow she raised her hand to acknowledge his presence before picking up her pace. Basil barked.

'Quiet,' she growled under her breath, 'he might take it as an invitation.'

'But Symon was by her side. 'You still go for a run every morning?' he asked.

'Yes.'

'May I join you?'

'You already have.'

'How are you, old boy?' He addressed Basil, as, behind her, he moved to her other side.

As he co-ordinated his stride with hers, Basil barked a friendly greeting and wagged his tail with delight. April simmered, searched for something disparaging to say to make her feel in control.

Symon had great legs, but they were no longer tanned. She said with feigned coolness, 'You obviously haven't been doing any running or beach combing. You've lost your colour and you sound a bit short of breath.'

To prove the point, she surged ahead, forgetting she had only resumed serious running herself yesterday. Soon Basil pulled her along. Symon caught up to her.

'You, too. Out of condition, I mean.' It wasn't a question rather a statement.

She stopped. Her chest rose and fell rapidly as she breathed. 'OK, I concede. I only started back yesterday. It's been too hot.'

He stopped, a yard of so ahead of her, mopping sweat from beneath the honey-gold hair which bounced over his forehead. Her gaze fell to his handsome features, his blue, sometimes aloof, eyes. But the early morning light revealed a few lines fanning from those eyes, and his mouth lacked the spontaneity it had once possessed. His was no longer an open, giving smile. The years of separation from Symons Hill had affected him.

After he left, she used to lay awake at night wondering where he was and what he was doing, who he was with. She'd wish he hadn't been that few years younger than she, tormented herself he'd gone looking for a younger, prettier woman and found one. And when The Run housekeeper, Millie, confirmed the rumour that he'd married, she'd worked to the point of exhaustion on the farm that she might sleep through the long nights.

Yet, he'd returned to The Hill alone and there had been no mention of a wife. Would she arrive soon? Would she ever arrive? Suppose they'd separated?

April continually reminded herself it was none of her business. But one day, soon, she'd ask the question, for she had a burning need to understand what he had never been man enough to disclose to her.

'A penny for them . . . ?'

April started at the sound of his voice, tossed her head. 'Offer me a thousand dollar fox-proof upgrade of my hen house and you might tempt me.' Basil's restlessness at her feet better indicated how she felt than did her phoney laugh.

'They need some work? I'd be happy to help — with my services, I mean. I'm afraid I haven't got any spare cash. Purchasing the store put my bank balance in the red.'

'Really? So the heir-apparent has a mortgage? No point in asking for a loan,' she muttered, and immediately regretted her impetuous remark.

He refused to acknowledge her unfortunate reference, though he jogged impatiently on the spot.

Embarrassed, she stepped off slowly and he followed.

'I was serious about my offer of help with the chicken house, by the way. Do let me know if I can do anything.' He jogged on. She only just heard his remark, 'You're looking more relaxed

114

this morning. Last night you seemed tired and out of sorts.'

The remark was clearly meant as a compliment — awkward, but pleasant. 'That's country life for you. Which direction are you taking when we get to the main road?' she asked as naturally as she could.

'I'm going to the post office. I want to check up on Essie to see how she is after her adventure. You too, I suppose.'

She'd almost nodded for indeed she had planned to do the same. 'Actually I'm taking the opposite direction.'

'Let me know what your committee decides tonight. I'm willing to talk to the members about the impossibility of operating from the building in its present condition, or they may prefer to consult the postal authorities. I'm hoping they'll see it's useless going into a battle that's already been lost.'

She tossed her head. 'I wouldn't bet on it. I'm sure we'll be in touch after the meeting.'

They'd arrived at the main road. As

they waited for a car to pass, she asked, 'How's your Grandfather?'

'He ought to be in hospital, but he refuses, insists on the doctor calling every day. How's your patient?'

'Twiggy's fine. I'd best be off.' Basil barked, tugging the lead in the direction they usually took towards the post office. She redirected him with a jerk. 'See you.'

'Perhaps I'll see you running again sometime?'

'I never go at the same time twice,' she replied hastily.

If he thought they could resume their morning jogs as if the last few years hadn't happened . . .

'I guess I'll catch up with you somewhere along the line.'

She watched him jog towards the small township. Another mistake. She should have hurried away before a sense of loss swept over her, but it did, and mesmerised, she observed his fluid movements and her heart yearned for what might have been.

How cool she would have felt had she been able to shout something flippant such as, 'Don't overdo it,' but instead her gaze lingered, taunting herself until he disappeared over an incline. And suddenly, she didn't quite understand why, moisture gathered in her eyes, tears trickled down her warm cheeks, and soon she wept openly.

'Blast!' she said to Basil between the sobs, forcing her legs forward in the opposite direction to Symon, leaving him behind, as he left her. 'Bother, bother, bother, I thought I'd done all my crying over that man.'

Basil wagged his tail, tugged on the lead, urging her to pick up the pace.

'Thanks, big boy.' She sniffed and mopped the remains of tears from her face with the back of her hand. 'Let's go.'

They turned for home. If she met any locals, they'd know immediately she'd been crying and probably guess why, and she had her reputation as an independent and successful woman to protect.

The thought coupled with her self-respect enabled her to work up the will to stem the tears, but only when she reached Gumbooya without meeting anyone did she breath easier.

* * *

After breakfast and feeding Twiggy and Jelly Bean, with Basil running behind, and Jelly Bean sitting cheekily on the seat beside her, she did her usual check around the property on her mini-tractor.

Seeing the hens idly pecking the ground, greeting old Topsy, who no longer gave milk, but had earned herself a comfortable retirement on the farm-let, and the thriving vegetable garden always empowered April.

Soon, bumping into Symon this morning had drifted from her thoughts. By the afternoon, absorbed in painting a yellow robin and planning for the evening meeting, his sudden reappearance no longer troubled her.

* * *

Rod Marsh arrived early for the *Save Our Post Office* meeting. He greeted her with a kiss on the cheek, handed her a small burgundy hard-covered book. 'I picked this up very cheaply at a second-hand book exchange in Booroondara.'

'A Norman Lindsay — *Halfway To Anywhere*,' she read from the cover. 'Thanks, but really, you must keep it. It's a real find.'

He looked flushed, as if embarrassed. 'I already have a copy,' he said.

She opened the book. 'It's in excellent condition. I'll pay you for it, of course.'

'It's a gift, April,' he said sharply. 'I bought it for your collection of Australian literature.'

Did accepting a gift from Rod give him ideas she didn't want him to have? 'It was very thoughtful of you.' She smiled. 'My treat the next time we go to dinner.'

She didn't hear his reply for the doorbell rang. The committee had arrived. Before settling down to the meeting, April invited them to meet Twiggy, but the cheeky young charmer, Jelly Bean, insisted on their attention, by loping across the sideboard, over-turning the fruit bowl and sending a spill of apples and bananas to the floor.

'It's time she learned she's a possum,' Majory Hamilton said, 'When do you plan releasing her back into the wild?'

'Soon. I'm waiting for the vet to give me the final OK.' April stroked the silky fur of the little marsupial, having caught her with ease. She had gained Jelly Bean's total trust, for she under-stood the trauma the little lady had been through.

'It gets harder to give them up by the week,' she added, smiling. 'Make yourselves comfortable and get started while I bed down our young show-off.'

A rough, but large and lined, timber lean-to attached to the house had been erected to accommodate and confine her native animals while they recovered from the loss of their mothers. Twiggy would be moved out there from the pantry as she developed. Placing the reluctant Jelly Bean inside, she gave her rump a gentle slap.

'No more mischief,' she scolded, her lips curving.

The meeting was underway, with Rod in the chair, when she returned to the dining room. They were discussing the condition of the post office, and had agreed the building must be saved. That meant restoration.

Marjory Hamilton, once legendary for her efforts on school committees, the pony club and the church, agreed to come out of retirement and head-up the fundraising committee to finance the rebuilding. Bob Daniels, a retired builder, offered to recruit volunteers and spearhead the restoration work.

The meeting progressed at a useful pace. It impressed April that everyone was so willing and dedicated, but she pointed out, 'We can't ignore the fact that restoring the post office will take a long time, and Ruth's dilemma requires an immediate answer. If Symon sticks to his position, he'll be advertising for a new postal officer within the week.'

The committee members were nodding their approval when the door bell sounded.

'It's probably Gerry,' Rod suggested. 'Ask him for his note for being late,' he jested, exaggerating his best school principal's voice as April hurried to the door. Basil trailed after her.

As she drew closer, an inexplicable knot of apprehension developed in her stomach. Basil barked, his tail wagged excitedly. No question who stood outside. Slowly she opened the door.

Symon's hair flounced across his forehead, shadowing his face, his eyes, but he appeared to be breathing hard. She felt slightly breathless herself as she stared at him with questioning eyes.

6

'Am I too late to speak at the meeting?' Symon asked. Why couldn't he have stayed away? Why did he have to keep reappearing at unexpected moments?

She shook her head, forced a steely scowl. 'You're unbelievable. I don't remember you being elected to the committee.'

'Ha ha. As if anyone would elect public enemy number one to your committee. I'm surprised the phone lines didn't drop out with all the talk about me that's gone on over the wires since I arrived home.'

A hint of guilt flashed into her head but as quickly vanished. She had nothing to feel guilty about. She tilted her head. 'So Symons' Hill is home for you again.'

'Sarcasm doesn't suit you, April. Did

I hear a yes to my request to address the meeting?'

April clipped hair behind her ear with uneasy fingers, felt the heat of embarrassment as it swept into her cheeks. If he hadn't caught her by surprise she might have dealt more maturely with his arrival.

Grow up, she told herself. Stick to the facts. Insulting him probably hurts you more than him.

'Sorry, Symon, but it's committee only. You can put whatever you have to say in a letter to our chairman, and it'll be considered, I assure you.'

'It will be too late.'

His persistence started to annoy her. 'Please Symon, write to the chairman — it's Rod Marsh.'

Now he sounded annoyed. 'How cosy. With you as secretary between the two of you you can control things at comfortable tête-a-têtes, eh?'

'You're being offensive.'

'I apologise.' It didn't sound like an apology. 'But we're wasting time here.

has your little clique found a way to help Ruth?'

'It's a committee, not a clique, and we were about to discuss it when you arrived.'

'I've got an idea which I believe could satisfy everyone's needs.'

'Give up Symon, and go home.'

'Be it on your head.'

He turned away as Gerry came up the drive, and addressed him.

'I didn't know you were coming, mate,' he said to Symon.

'Me neither,' April managed to fit in before the men almost brushed her aside as they entered the house.

Fuming, she followed, planning her next move. She'd stick to meeting procedure and challenge his right to invade the meeting under committee rules. The other members would support her.

Bob Daniels questioned him immediately. 'Andrews, to what do we owe the pleasure of your company?'

Symon pushed his hair from his

forehead. 'I apologise for the intrusion, but I've been giving Ruth's position a lot of thought and I think I can see a way out for her.'

'Look son, we know you're a Symons, but that doesn't give you a mortgage on problem solving. If your idea's so good, how come no-one here thought about it?' said a sceptical Daniels.

'Did you invite him here, April?' Rod asked.

April stood by her chair, her cheeks pink, her eyes clouded. Uncomfortable, Symon thought. Perhaps she recalled what he'd said earlier about the biased attitude of people to him because of his name.

How he hankered to spike their prejudices with a few forceful, well chosen words, but the moment required diplomacy, not aggression for his idea at least deserved to be considered.

'Of course I didn't. I . . . '

Predicting she'd suggest he be tossed out, deny him, he chipped in, 'It's a committee decision, surely. Do I get a hearing, or do I leave?'

April's voice sounded uncertain but resigned. 'Rod, since he's here, I vote we hear Mr Andrews out. It's doubtful it can have any influence on what we decide.' And, as if troubled by her words, she dragged out her chair and flopped into it.

Her motion drew general agreement. Marjory Hamilton commented, 'He organised the search for Essie. We owe him for that.'

Rod glared at her, obviously not pleased at the reminder. 'OK Andrews, let's hear what you have to say.'

Symon moved to the head of the table, stood behind the chairman, where the attention of all committee members focused on him. 'You've been looking at the problem from only one angle instead of . . .'

'Get on with it,' Daniel growled.

'Simply put, had anyone thought of setting up a roster of people willing to sit with Essie or take her to their home for the day?'

'You mean hand the old lady around like a parcel with a no fixed address label?' Gerry rushed in. 'Poor old thing. A drover's dog can see that wouldn't fix anything.'

Symon flourished his hands with impatience, retorted sharply, 'Hutter, you've got the brai . . . '

He saw April shake her head and quickly regained his cool. 'You underestimate a drover's dog. They're smart. Give the idea some thought, mate, before you can it.'

'I can see the possibilities . . . ' Rod began.

'If you'd let me finish, you'll all see the possibilities. At the moment Ruth has the responsibility for her mother's well-being twenty-four hours a day. A daily roster system of people who know and care about her, would leave Ruth free to accept my offer to run the post office from the store. It would also give her a break from the constant need to monitor Essie's movements and a degree of respite care.'

He waited for their reaction, but his plan appeared to render them speechless. Silence. And, as suddenly, everyone spoke at once.

Rod called for order, addressed April, 'What do you think? You're closest to Ruth. Would she go for the idea?'

'I'm wondering why it didn't occur to anyone? We're a close-knit community and yet, in our eagerness to help, we didn't think around the problem. Symon was right about that. I, for one, think it's an excellent idea, and I'm sure Ruth will welcome it. She's been looking really tired lately,' April acknowledged.

Rod acted immediately. 'Very well, sit down, Andrews, while we take a vote.'

Symon shrugged at the formality of it all, but crossed to the window seat.

'Is it the wish of the meeting that we put the plan to Ruth for her agreement? Show of hands, please,' Rod asked.

Glancing around, he said in a harsh

tone, 'Please note I'm abstaining, but the motion is carried.'

Not for the first time, Symon sensed Rod resented him. He'd thought back at the hall when Essie went missing, the man didn't like being sidelined from the search. But now he reasoned, his antipathy had clearly more to do with April. He probably believed Symon had returned to The Hill to reclaim her.

Symon decided to look for the right opportunity to assure him that wasn't the case. If Rod could make her happy, he wanted it as much as anyone.

Daniels began speaking. 'We should explain to Andrews that we haven't been sitting here tonight twiddling our thumbs. We've put plans in place to preserve the post office because it's part of Symons Hill's heritage.'

'That's fine. So long as you understand it can't operate as a post office after next Friday.'

'I think we've got that message, mate.' Gerry stood up. 'Sorry I have to leave, got the mother-in-law staying for a few days. Put the wife and me down for the roster. We're happy to take a turn.'

April agreed to contact Ruth, and with her approval and help, the Thorpes were appointed to draw up a roster of responsible and understanding people to care for Essie.

'I can handle the post office at weekends,' Symon said. 'That'll give Ruth time to spend with her mother.'

'And I work from home, so she can come here once a week if that helps. She can feed the animals, and sit by me while I paint,' April volunteered.

Rod closed the proceedings after confirming people who had to take action, and announcing the date and venue for the next meeting.

'If Ruth agrees to the plan,' April told Steve Thorpe as he headed for the door, 'I'll take Essie for the first few days until the schedule settles down.'

Symon didn't quite know what got into him, but he found himself standing behind April's chair, his hands on her shoulders, saying, 'I hope this community appreciates you, April Showe . . . Stewart. Your warm and generous heart bowls me over.'

Bob Daniels stood up, eye-balled him. 'You're asking us if we appreciate her. You've got a nerve.'

'And a short memory,' Steve chipped in.

He'd asked for it, felt as uncomfortable as hell, a contagion in a town where the people cared for each other, but had left him out of the loop.

'Please,' April pushed back her chair, came to her feet. 'We've had a useful meeting. Let's forget our differences over a cup of tea. I'll put on the kettle.'

'I'll do it. You talk to your friends,' Symon said, making his way to the kitchen, determined not to accept any argument from her. After filling and switching on the kettle, he prepared to return, but stopped when he heard slightly raised voices.

'You're sure it's OK to leave you alone with Andrews?'

It wasn't hard to recognise Rod Marsh's voice.

'Why on earth not? I don't understand why you're bothered.'

'Me neither,' he said in a dull voice. 'It's obvious I'm wasting my time. I'll see you around.'

'I'll call you tomorrow. It's been a good result tonight, Rod. And a lot of credit goes to you for being such a decisive chairman.' She sounded as if she were trying hard to be nice.

When Symon heard the front door close he returned to the sitting room.

'They've all left. You certainly know how to clear a room,' she said, her eyes lifeless.

'Can I help being the town's baddie?' A smile might be in order, he thought. It had no affect. She looked tired, disinterested.

'Look, I'm sorry. I shouldn't have come. Back there, I had no right . . . ' He braced himself, clamped his feet to the floor, preparing for a blast, as she

133

waved her hand in a jaded, dismissive gesture.

'Forget it. I should be congratulating you. You've probably solved our problem.'

Stirred by her unexpected tolerance, he said quietly, 'Considering I caused the crisis in the first place, I felt obligated to find an acceptable solution for Ruth.'

She turned wearily to leave the room, before swinging back again to say, 'You should know we agreed at the meeting with your assessment that the post office couldn't have operated in its present condition for much longer. One or two of the members did think you could have warned us of your plans, though.'

He shrugged. 'I wasn't sure where Australia Post negotiations were with Ruth.'

The shrill of the boiling kettle broke into the tense-filled room.

She surprised him by saying, 'Stay for a cup of tea. I made some Anzac biscuits and need someone to eat them.'

The kettle turned itself off. He smiled. 'Anzac biscuits? I haven't had home-made biscuits in yonks. You might be sorry you mentioned them.'

He insisted she sit down and took control in the kitchen, poured the tea. 'Weak, black as usual?' he asked.

Her tired eyes brightened. She nodded, her pony tail swung engagingly, before settling over one shoulder.

'So what changes are you planning at the store?' she asked as they returned to the sitting room, he carrying two mugs of tea, she a plate of biscuits.

'It can't survive by selling a few newspapers and cartons of milk, that's for sure. And I can't rely on people's good intentions or their loyalty to the town. In the end they'll travel to the regional centres to buy their weekly supplies because it's cheaper.'

'So how do you compete?'

'A small, inexpensive café, home-made scones, cookies, that kind of thing. Busloads of retirees, weekend tourists who drive to the hills for a day out, pass through Symons Hill without a second glance. What is there to see? A few tired old shops, a quaint little church, a post of . . . ' He stopped suddenly. 'On second thoughts, I don't think I'll go down that path.'

She smiled gently.

'Suffice to say the day-trippers and weekenders are on their way to nearby villages which did their market research and know what encourages people to stop off.'

'You sound as if you've done some research yourself?'

'I didn't buy the store on a whim. Naturally I did my homework first. I'm going to give pulling in the day-trippers a good old college try. We'll serve coffee, light lunches, set up an outdoor garden area for the warmer weather, organise tours of our mud brick houses. Then there's the primary school. Kids and teachers need nourishing lunches. I'm planning an order and deliver service. That, of course, is if I can persuade Rod Marsh to co-operate.

'I'm not his favourite person at the moment.'

'Oh?' she queried with raised brows, 'What have you done to him?'

'He sees me as a rival for your affections. Surely you've picked that up?'

'Nonsense, he knows you're married.'

April's hand shot to her mouth as the words slipped out, and she waited, breathless for his response. But he helped himself to another biscuit and said nothing.

After what felt like a century of silence, she stopped waiting for an answer and said, with a hint of admiration in her voice, 'I can hear the enthusiasm for reviving the store in your voice, but it sounds like a lot of long hard hours on the job.'

'Hard work doesn't worry me, but I've messed up so many other things in my life, I'm determined to make this new enterprise work.'

She looked up sharply, wondering

what he meant, but as he dusted a crumb from his jeans, she saw only that his movement appeared strained.

'If it doesn't, we might have to set up a 'Save Our Store' committee,' she commented lightly to ease the tension.

It failed to draw even the suggestion of a positive response.

'If my investment fails I'll know I haven't done my job properly. And anyone trying to save the store would be wasting their energy on a lost cause.'

She stood up, drained by the events of the evening.

'Time will tell,' and stifling a yawn, she added. 'Sorry, Symon, but that discussion is for another day, and it's Twiggy time again. Can you see yourself out?'

7

It was the day before Ruth started work in the store. April had spoken to her about Symon's idea of her friends helping out by caring for Essie. As the plan became clear to Ruth, her care-worn face had eased and a sob slowed her voice as she'd gratefully agreed to the plan.

'What are friends for,' April had said, vaguely tearful herself.

As first on the list of carers, she rang Ruth on Sunday to arrange to pick up Essie next morning after her jog.

Next she rang to ask Charles Bransgrove, the veterinarian from the nearest large town, to call and check on Twiggy, who continued to thrive. Hair had started to cover her and she was experimenting with ways to slip out of the makeshift cloth pouch.

April had become known in the area

for rescuing and raising orphan native animals at their most vulnerable stage. It could be quite expensive, for the milk they drank had to be specially made-up, but who cared when you had the exhilaration and reward of seeing them returned in good health to their natural environment?

'The vet's due this afternoon to check you out,' she told Twiggy at feed time. 'But you've got a long way to go before we say goodbye.' She touched her on her damp nose. 'Now stay out of mischief while I'm on my rounds of the farm. Soon you'll be able to join us.'

Outside, as customary, she climbed on to her mini-tractor. Basil leapt on to the seat beside her and she activated the motor. They set off around the perimeter of the property to inspect the fences for break-ins by rabbits or foxes who prowled the bushland in increasing numbers. But her mind wasn't on the job, particularly when they reached the fence over which Symon used to climb in those early days of their friendship.

Briefly, her concentration lapsed, long enough for her to miss a tree stump. The front wheels of her tractor reared, the machine stalled, shuddered and sent her sprawling on to the ground.

'I can't believe this,' she muttered, dragging herself into a sitting position, brushing leaves and twigs from her hair and clothes.

Having caught her breath, she rolled up the right leg of her jeans to inspect any damage. Interested, Basil panted over her grazed knee, his tongue lolling out.

She swiped at him with her hand. 'It's not funny you stupid dog. You're supposed to protect me. Why didn't you warn me?' she moaned, 'It hurts.'

And cross with herself, she tried to stand up, but the minute she put weight on her right foot, a stab of pain rifled through her causing her to sink back on to the forest floor of spent leaves and bark.

'Dear Heaven,' she groaned, 'how on

141

earth am I going to get back to the house?'

Basil barked and ran off.

'That's right,' she called after him, 'leave me for dead.' And then to herself she muttered, 'Can't blame him. It's my own stupid fault, day-dreaming over that insensitive Symon Andrews. If I were Basil, I'd sooner be chasing rabbits than listening to a disgruntled woman.'

She took a few deep breaths and assessed the situation. The tractor wasn't too far away. If she could get across to it, and use her bottom to dislodge it from the stump, maybe it would start.

Using the palms of her hands and her tail, she slid slowly towards the machine, but the harder she worked, the farther away it seemed. Her hands were scratched and sweaty, her tail burning from the effort.

She paused, looked around her for another option. If she wriggled to the nearest tree, she could use it to haul herself to her feet and then with a bit of luck, hop from tree to tree until she reached the machine.

Squirming and twisting, hot and irritable, she came within a long arm's reach of her destination when, from behind her, she heard Basil returning, barking merrily.

'How very considerate of you to come back,' she mocked without looking around.

'No trouble at all,' said the deep, low voice she knew so well.

Her problems faded from her mind and with a grunt she reached for the tree trunk, dragged herself up and swung around on her good ankle.

'What are you doing here?'

He patted the dog.

'Basil dropped in, didn't you mate, and gave me the message that you needed help, but if we got it wrong, I'll leave.'

He turned away and began walking towards the fence.

She took a step forward, stifled a yelp

of pain, and sank to the ground. Sprawled there, she yelled, 'Symon Andrews, don't you dare go off and leave me. Come back this minute.'

He spun around. 'If you're sure?'

She saw the teasing twinkle in his sometimes aloof blue eyes, and said petulantly. 'It's not funny,' but she was starting to see the humour in it.

'From where I stand, it is. You look a mess. You remind me of the time when we were kids and . . . '

She broke in, unwilling to hear the reminiscence. 'A mess?' she cried. 'Do you think I don't know how I look? But thanks, anyway. I'm absolutely in the mood for compliments.'

'Any time.' Laughter lines fanned from his eyes. His smile was its once generous self.

Even in her dilemma, at that moment, she thought she'd rediscovered something of the Symon she'd loved.

'Don't you care that I've probably broken my leg?' She exaggerated hoping to mask the undercurrent of her feelings.

'At least you wouldn't be able to call any protest meetings for a while.' He approached her. 'Let me take a look.'

He knelt beside her before she had time to decide whether or not to protest. Gently, but clinically, he ran his hand over her leg, working up to her knee and back to her ankle.

She preached to herself that this man was any man, but his nearness made her uncomfortably hot. She needed words, said the first which came into her head. 'You smell of turpentine.'

'The cost of aftershave is terribly expensive these days.'

She laughed. 'I was painting earlier. I probably smell of it myself.'

'You smell of soap and sunshine and . . . earth.'

Ridiculously pleased, she fingered the flush of pleasure which broke out on her face, asked, 'Have you been painting?'

'Only shelf fittings for the post office

section of the store. I'm going up to install them later today. No need to remind you Ruth starts tomorrow?'

She slapped the palm of her hand to her head. With him around the important things had a tendency to drift right out of her mind.

'If there's anything wrong with my knee or ankle, I don't know . . . '

'Let's not panic. Put your arm around my waist, I'll grip you under the shoulders and you can lean on me while we get across to the tractor.'

'I suppose I'll live,' she ventured, curving her mouth. What a sight she must look.

'Guaranteed.'

His arm wound protectively under her shoulders, she leaned into his body for support and without meaning to, surrendered to his strength. It felt reassuring, protective . . . She dare not think beyond that.

'Ever carried a sack of potatoes before?' she quipped.

'You're as light as fairy floss.'

146

A smile teased her lips. The pressure on her foot seemed to ease.

★ ★ ★

They reached the tractor after several slow steps, and gripping her on both sides of her waist, Symon eased her into the passenger seat of the tractor.

With Basil as escort, he drove the vehicle slowly, scanned her face when they traversed rough ground for any signs of pain.

She tried to meet his concerned glances with reassuring looks, but occasionally a small cry escaped her lips.

She began to suspect her injury might need more than ice packs and overnight rest. And to worry that she wouldn't be able to care for Essie tomorrow.

★ ★ ★

When they reached the house, he sprang from the vehicle, placed one arm

147

under her knees and another under her arms, lifted her from the motor and carried her into the house. In the sitting-room, he lowered her gently on to the old sofa.

'I'll phone the doctor and ask him to call,' he said.

She laughed mockingly. 'You've been away a long time, haven't you? Doctors don't do house calls any more.'

'Old Simpson calls on Grandfather.'

'When Cyrus Symons speaks, everyone jumps. I don't have that effect, except maybe on Basil.' She stroked the dog as he nuzzled up to her. 'You did well bringing help. Good boy.'

'You're glad I found you?'

She bit on her lip, nodded, 'Didn't I say thanks? I meant to.'

He filled the kettle. 'Do I phone the doctor?'

She glanced at her watch. 'Charles Bransgrove's due any time. He can look at the foot and give me some idea if it's a matter of life or death.'

'Bransgrove the vet?'

She smiled at the tone of his voice. 'He's popping in to give Twiggy the once-over. He can advise me. I'm expecting him to say, 'put a cold compress on your ankle, take two paracetamol and rest overnight'.'

'Is cleaning up smudges on the face also part of the vet's treatment, or would you like me do it?'

Her hand flew to her hot cheek. 'Thanks, but no. I'd be grateful if you could bring me a damp face cloth.'

He grinned. 'Done.'

As he started to move from the room, she added, 'Would you also mind getting me a packet of frozen peas from the freezer?'

'Hungry are you?'

She should have laughed but, in pain, her endurance was being sorely tested. 'Forget it, I can manage,' she said swinging her feet to the floor. But her ankle refused to support her and she sank back into the sofa.

Circumstances seemed to be conspiring against her, throwing them together.

If she wasn't careful she could fall in love all over again.

'Give me a break, April. For once in your life let someone do something for you. You, young woman, need to learn that accepting help with grace and gratitude when it's offered is appreciated. Throwing it back in people's faces and uncompromising independence can really be a big turn-off.'

'But . . . ' The protest on her lips faltered as the significance of his statement started to take root.

'No buts.'

He rustled in the freezer, pulled out a packet of peas, loosened them inside their packaging with a few heavy thumps. 'Now what?'

'Wrap them in a hand towel. They make an excellent ice pack.'

Fascinated by his efficiency, she recalled the first day her mother took her to the big house to 'learn how the best kitchens operate'.

She and Symon had already formed an edgy friendship, but it had been their secret, for her mother had warned her not to encourage the boy from the big house.

He'd popped his head around the corner of the kitchen and watched. Huh, she'd thought, he's a useless boy, he won't be interested.

But she'd challenged, 'If you're going to stand there gawping, you might as well do something.'

He'd put one foot inside, had one eye on her mother. She warned him, 'Make yourself scarce, boy, before your mother finds you,' but he'd said she was out and complained of boredom.

As usual her mother softened to his smile, slapped a cheerful kiss on his chubby cheek and relented.

'All right, you can stay, but keep the noise down. Your grandfather would give me my marching orders if he knew.'

April used to wonder, mildly envious, why her mother fussed over Symon, but hardly ever over her. She suspected it had something to do with her choosing to stay at the city school and live with her father when her parents separated.

*　★　*

Symon's chubby cheeks had long-since disappeared, but he still had a killer of a smile when he chose — one which not only charmed middle-aged housekeepers, she thought with a touch of pleasure.

'Something amusing you?' he asked. 'Care to share it?'

She raised her brows. 'I was thinking about a certain small boy and how he learned his practical skills.'

'Lay back,' he growled. 'I've taken enough lip from you today.'

Gently he lifted her ankle and wrapped it into the bed of frozen peas. 'Next, a cup of tea and two paracetamols.'

If he didn't leave, she could find herself wallowing in a mire of memories. 'I'm not in any pain. I just want to sleep.'

'OK, I can take a hint, but I don't want to leave you alone at the minute. I'll phone Mrs Daniels. She may be able to pop around later.'

'I'm not sick, Symon. I can still talk and use a phone.' Her heart, her pride wouldn't let her accept any more from him.

He clicked his fingers. 'Hey, I've thought of the very thing.' He moved towards the door, pointed his finger at her, 'Now, don't you run away. I'll be back.'

'Alas, I'll be here, count on it.'

Basil bounded off after Symon.

'Traitor,' she called, before sighing. What was she going to do with Essie tomorrow? Even if she felt a lot better, should the old lady decide to wander off . . . She picked up the portable phone and rang the Thorpes.

They agreed to rearrange the roster and take April's turn. Next she rang Ruth and, downplaying her mishap, informed her of the change in plans. And with that off her mind, she dropped back on to the sofa and tried to relax.

Her mouth felt dry, her ankle ached. What had caused Symon to dash off, she wondered in a fog of drowsiness as she lay back into the pillows and closed her eyes.

8

'Is anyone home?' The vet's cheery call woke her. She sat up with a start and brushed at her hair. 'Come in, Charles. I'm in the sitting room.'

He was a big man, fortyish, a determined jawline, touches of grey at the sides of his dark hair. When he smiled his face puckered engagingly. 'Where's the patient?' he asked.

April dragged in a breath. She'd been so wrapped up in her own misfortune, she'd forgotten about Twiggy. She swung her feet to the floor, but didn't risk standing up.

'She's in her pouch in the pantry,' she said. 'Er . . . I've had a minor accident. Would you mind getting her? She'll be hungry.'

'Stay there. I'll find her.'

He brought Twiggy out. 'Hold her while I give her the once over. She looks fine, though. I'm more concerned about you. You're a whiter shade of pale as the old song says.' His face creased, his eyes twinkled.

She smiled, watched as he tested Twiggy's limbs, ran experienced hands over the 'roo's body.

'What happened to you? Ran into trouble at the protest meeting, eh?'

She tossed her head, laughed, and then remembered Symon's reference to smudges and scrubbed away at her face.

'I came off the tractor. I think I've sprained my ankle. Could you give me your professional opinion?'

A confusion of sounds from the back door captured their attention. 'My diagnosis is she needs to rest, Charles. But she takes no notice of me. Maybe you can persuade her.' Symon stood by the sitting room entrance.

'Ignore him,' April said, 'that's what I'm doing.'

Charles raised his eyebrows. 'Afternoon, Andrews,' he said before popping

Twiggy into her lap and lifting her legs back on to the sofa.

A few questions followed before he probed cautiously around the ankle area. When she responded painfully to his touch, he said no more than, 'Ah ha.'

Straightening up, he warned, 'I'm afraid you're not going anywhere for a while, April. You'll have to see the Doc and have it X-rayed, but my guess is you have a stress fracture.'

Though she'd been trying to prepare herself for this worst-case scenario, she groaned. 'But my animals . . . '

Symon moved into the room. Took Twiggy from her. 'It's OK. If necessary, I'll be around to feed the animals, but look what I've brought you. It'll get you around the house anywhere, any time.'

She turned as he gestured towards the door. A motorised wheelchair stood in the entrance.

She stared at it. 'You expect me to use that?'

'I've brought crutches, too. They're

old props that Grandfather's recently discarded in favour of his bed.' Symon's eyes glinted with challenge.

'Well done, Andrews. Now calm down, girl. At least you'll be able to get around,' Charles said. 'If you like I'll take the joey and Jelly Bean to the wild life shelter in the next town.'

Symon answered for her. 'No need.' He stroked Twiggy. 'Uncle Symon's going to look after you, and the other animals, isn't he?'

'Good, and can you get April to the doctor, Andrews?'

April looked at Charles and then across to Symon, a protest on her lips, but in time she remembered his jibe about accepting help graciously. 'I can't resist two handsome guys at once. I'm waving the white flag, here,' she said lightly, and an immediate sense of relief swept over her.

After Charles left, Symon rang the medical centre and insisted on an immediate appointment with the doctor. 'The wheelchair or crutches and my arm out to the car?' he asked.

She surprised herself. 'Your arm, please. I'm still on L plates for driving the wheelchair.'

* * *

The X-rays confirmed the stress fracture, her foot and leg to her knee were placed in plaster, and her active life put on hold.

From the wheelchair, or on crutches, she could care for herself and paint, but Symon came daily to feed the outside animals. And with his encouragement, she learned to laugh at her awkwardness, her dilemma, and to accept his help. And, like Ruth, that of the Symons Hill community.

Symon moved her easel so that it caught the late autumn sun filtering through the window. He helped her outside and together they watched Twiggy take her first tentative hops. 'She's doing better than me,' she commented, and they laughed.

But her heart felt troubled by the reawakening of her feelings for him, and by the fact that not once had he mentioned his wife, or indeed where she was. And, fearing the truth, she continued to leave the question unasked.

Occasionally the light of hope eased the ache in her heart — one day he might be free to marry her. Occasionally realism dashed these hopes. He'd given her no indication that he had more than feelings of friendship for her.

At last the plaster on her leg came off, and her ankle felt strong enough to enable her to resume normal activities. Essie came on Tuesdays, and together they roamed around April's small farm, talking to the animals, collecting eggs, picking the late vegetables.

In the afternoon Essie usually fell asleep in the rocking chair, occasionally they visited Ruth at the counter of the post office, or went driving into the nearest big town. With the old lady in her care, April stayed constantly on alert and appreciated even more the strain her friend, Ruth, had been operating under.

But for the remainder of the week, the house felt empty. Basil's bark seemed mournful, the chickens squabbled and Twiggy scratched at the door to get out. Symon had spoken of The Run as sad after her mother left for home in the afternoons. With Symon's exodus, empty was a better word for her cottage right now.

She talked up the idea that in time she'd forget the pleasant, sharing days with him during her convalescence and get back into a routine. She accepted extra shifts caring for Essie, and helped with the painting of the renovated post office building which, under the committee's revised plan, was to become a museum and craft shop. Ruth would run it at weekends to attract day-trippers to the area.

A win-win situation everyone agreed.

Slowly, April recommenced her daily jogging routine with Basil, searched with a hopeful heart for Symon to emerge from the back entrance to The Run. He didn't come. He clearly avoided her at every opportunity.

Life wasn't happening for her with any degree of satisfaction. She felt restless, as if marking time, waiting for something to happen. As she struggled with the painting of the long, hooked beak of an eastern spinebill, Basil stretched, got up from the mat and sauntered out. She heard the familiar closing of the back door, Basil bark in response. And she knew with certainty that Symon had come.

Stay cool, don't get up, act naturally, she implored herself. But her hand tensed around the slender handle of the paint brush.

And when she looked up, her heart leapt. Symon stood in the doorway.

Denying the impulse to throw herself into his arms and weep at his return, her voice stumbled over the words, 'Symon, how nice.'

And only then did she notice the pain-filled eyes which stared back at her. She ran to him, placed her hands on his arm. 'Symon, what is it? What's happened?'

'Grandfather died early this morning.'

'I'm truly sorry. Can I help? I know you didn't always get on, but you loved him.'

'He was my only family.' He dropped into a chair. 'Can you be there for me?'

'Of course. You were there for me when I hurt my ankle. But what else can I do? Perhaps help you with the funeral arrangements?'

He nodded. 'It's all done.'

'Then let me ring around to tell people. I suppose your wife will come home? Have you contacted her yet?'

He ran a hand over his forehead, forced back his hair. 'You'll have to know some time. I haven't got a wife.'

9

'But . . . but . . . Millie said . . . ' April cried. A shadow passed across his face. He flourished his hands. 'Please, now's not the time to talk about it.'

'Then you're separated?' She couldn't let it go.

'April, it's in the past. Maybe later I can explain everything.' Again he raked hair back from his forehead.

April backed off, the futility of pressing him obvious for the moment. 'Remember we go way back. When you're ready to talk, I'm here. Have you decided on hymns for the service, a sprig of rosemary perhaps for the gathering? I have a rosemary bush if you like the idea.'

He shook his head. 'Cyrus arranged everything before he died. All I had to do, could do, was ring the doctor and the funeral director.'

'I hate that. It gives the family that's left behind nothing to do during their most vulnerable time.'

'You understand?'

'Of course. I've always thought arranging the funeral should be part of the grieving period.'

'You're a remarkable lady, April Showers.'

Her heart lightened. A thought she'd never believed possible before began to take hold. She and Symon could be friends, and it comforted her that though her dream of being his wife had ended, she didn't have to cut herself off entirely from him.

'Stay there. I'll make you a coffee.'

★ ★ ★

Symon called again a couple of weeks after the funeral. To her surprise, April noticed he'd regained the spring in his step, the resonance in his voice.

'Will you stay on at The Run, or sell it?' she asked as she continued painting.

He watched over her shoulder, her brush strokes grew uncertain under his appraisal, his nearness. She paused to replenish the brush in a dab of blue paint from her palette.

'The wrens are exquisite,' he said. 'Remember Buttons and Jenny?'

'Fondly,' she said, 'they were delightful little visitors to the garden.'

The room became silent. She continued to work, though the brushstrokes erred as she wondered if he'd come to talk about his marriage.

'Er, did you ask me something?' he said.

His mind seemed to be on something else. 'Now you've inherited The Run, do you intend to move into the big house?'

'No. The property isn't mine.'

'But surely . . . I mean, everyone knew you were Cyrus's heir.'

'And that's what the will said, but morally I couldn't accept his money. I've gifted everything to the State to be used for homeless and deprived children.'

April's hand jerked, a blue brush stroke shot up the paper. She swung around to face him. 'You're what?'

'I'm giving the Symons' money to the State. Do you have a problem with that?'

From her stool she stretched up and threw her arms around him. 'Oh Symon, what a truly magnificent thing to do. Has anyone told you lately how wonderful you are?'

'No-one who matters.' A small smile touched his lips. 'Friends again?'

'Friends,' she repeated, with new-found confidence. If she couldn't have his love, she'd settle for his friendship.

'Is your painting urgent, or can you stop working for a while to talk?'

Her heart skipped a beat. 'It's not that urgent.'

He placed his arm around her, led her to the sofa. Her heart now beat at a lively pace. 'What are we going to talk about?'

'I never thought it would be possible, but I can at last tell you why I left The Hill.'

'Ah ha — the missing link,' she murmured, sitting taut on the edge of the sofa, impatient to learn the truth, yet troubled that it might close the chapter on their renewed friendship.

He raked back his hair. 'This is so hard, almost unbelievable. I'm still wondering if it's all really happened.'

'Try it on me,' she prompted.

'Three years ago I informed Grandfather I planned to ask you to marry me.'

April stirred on her seat but remained silent.

'He blew up, refused to even countenance it. I told him I didn't need or want his blessing. I intended to marry you, anyway. That's when he produced the letter.'

She turned her eyes to meet his. 'What letter?'

'The letter from your mother agreeing to give her baby to my mother, who couldn't have children of her own. In return she was to receive this small acreage which is now yours. Cyrus said I was that baby, the result of a brief affair between Jean and my wayward father.'

'Surely that cannot be,' April cried. 'That would mean you're not a Symons, and we're . . . Dear Heaven, I can't bear to think about it.'

'That's why I left without any explanation. I couldn't go on living in the same town, loving you as I did, seeing you every day, not able to be with you. I prayed you'd come to despise me for deserting you and find happiness with someone else.'

April stood up, walked across to the window on spongy legs and gazed out upon the carpet of late autumn leaves, trying to process the implications of what she'd heard, speechless to express the turmoil within.

He came to her side, but she refused to acknowledge his presence until she felt his hands upon her shoulders, heard the soothing tone of his voice.

'It's going to be all right, April.'

'How can you even think that?'

'Come and sit down again. There's more to the story.'

In her heart April knew Symon wasn't in any way to blame and had acted with integrity, but she had to lash out at someone and he was there.

'I don't want to hear it. Tell it to your wife, wherever she is.'

'I told you I haven't got a wife — I've never been married. That's another story Cyrus invented to explain my sudden departure. And when I came back I found it convenient not to deny it. I wouldn't have told you all this now if I didn't feel free to do so.'

She swung around and stared at him. 'Another of Cyrus's stories? What?'

'Since Grandfather died, I've been going through his papers, and I discovered a few very interesting things. For example, your mother paid off her small acreage by working overtime at the big house.

'Cyrus's story that she received it in return for giving up her baby didn't quite crystallise in my mind. So I contacted the solicitor who was supposed to have drawn up the agreement and arranged everything legally.

'The document is a fake, as was your mother's signature on it. I compared it with the agreement she signed to buy the land. And this morning I had the news I've been waiting for. My legal adviser confirmed my birth mother as Cecily. There can be no doubting it.'

April felt queasy in the stomach, unable to process the detail of Symon's words. She flopped into a chair.

'But it doesn't make any sense. Why would he make up such a wicked story about my mother and your father?'

'You'd have to have lived with Grandfather to understand what drove him, and even so, it wasn't always possible to read him. He convinced me.' He shook his head. 'If I'd taken the time to think it through, instead of letting my emotions get in the way, I'd

171

have seen right through his nasty little scheme.

'His daughter had married beneath her with unfortunate consequences, so he was determined that I, as his heir, marry into a family of note and rebuild the Symons tradition of wealth and power.'

'And you foiled all his plans by falling for the daughter of the housekeeper? If it wasn't so tragic I'd laugh,' she said quietly.

'When I made it clear to him he couldn't stop me from marrying you, his devious mind dreamed up the slanderous story to prevent that happening, and succeeded. I should have used my head and reasoned that he'd never have named me as his heir if I didn't have Symons' blood.

'He'd sooner have left his estate to the lost dogs. But I swallowed the pitch so readily because it had an element of validity. Jean fussed over me far more than my mother and made me feel really loved and special. She could have been my mother.

'Sometimes it annoyed me that she seemed to love you more than me, but then I'd recall that she'd lost a dearly loved younger brother when he was a child. I think you reminded her of him. My mum had good taste. You're not hard to love.'

April edged closer to him, at last beginning to focus beyond the injustice done to Symon to the future — their future — and slowly happiness began to clear her mind and sweep away all the doubts. The missing link was finally in place.

'April,' he folded her in his arms, whispered into her hair, 'how can I make up to you for everything I've put you through?'

'If you're absolutely, positively sure you're not married, you can ask me to be your wife.'

He lifted her mouth to his. She tasted the sweetness of his lips, her eyes glazed with tears of joy.

'Oh darling, I can't believe it,' he said.

She brushed the hair back from his forehead and laced her arms lovingly around his neck.

★ ★ ★

In the damp early morning, under a leaden winter sky, they stood on the perimeter of the national park. Their breath emerged as steam, their leather boots scrunched into the faded leaves of autumn, as they jogged on the spot to keep warm. Basil, secured on his leash, scratched restlessly in the forest floor.

'You're free, Twiggy. Off you go,' April whispered, giving the kangaroo an endearing pat and a hefty shove on her considerable rump.

Over three feet tall, Twiggy hopped a few paces before looking back, uncertainly. And then, perhaps realising what lay ahead, she loped off, her tail bounding in unison with her long hind legs. At the edge of the trees, she hesitated once more as if saying goodbye, and disappeared into the woods.

'Goodbye, Twiggy. Come visit some time,' April called, before turning misty eyes up to Symon. 'This is the best part — returning the injured animals to the wild, to freedom.'

His arm circled her waist. 'And we have our freedom, too.'

Nothing could hide the sunshine in her heart as she reached to turn the collar of Symon's coat up around his ears and warm his cold lips with a kiss.

'I can't help it,' she explained. 'I've got three years to make up for doing without you.'

He slipped his hands beneath the hood of her jacket, cupped her face and placed his lips on hers. 'And the rest of your life to do it. Let's go home.'

We do hope that you have enjoyed reading this large print book.

Did you know that all of our titles are available for purchase?

We publish a wide range of high quality large print books including:
Romances, Mysteries, Classics
General Fiction
Non Fiction and Westerns

Special interest titles available in large print are:
The Little Oxford Dictionary
Music Book, Song Book
Hymn Book, Service Book

Also available from us courtesy of Oxford University Press:
Young Readers' Dictionary
(large print edition)
Young Readers' Thesaurus
(large print edition)

For further information or a free brochure, please contact us at:
Ulverscroft Large Print Books Ltd.,
The Green, Bradgate Road, Anstey,
Leicester, LE7 7FU, England.
Tel: (00 44) **0116 236 4325**
Fax: (00 44) **0116 234 0205**

Other titles in the
Linford Romance Library:

FORSAKING ALL OTHERS

Jane Carrick

Dr Shirley Baxter, after several inexcusable mistakes, leaves her London hospital to look after her sick grandfather in Inverdorran. However, with the help of locum Dr Andrews, he soon recovers. Shirley meets and falls in love with Neil Fraser who is working hard to build a local leisure centre. But Neil's plans are beset with problems, and after he suffers a breakdown, Shirley finds her medical training is once again in demand.

FORBIDDEN LOVE

Zelma Falkiner

By the time Lyndal Frazer learns the identity of the stranger who rescued her and her sheepdog, Rowdy, from drowning, it is too late. She has fallen half in love with a sworn enemy of her ailing father. Torn between growing attraction and duty, Lyndal chooses family loyalty. But Hugh Trevellyn has made up his mind, too; a bitter feud will not be allowed to come between them.